SHORT SHORT
STORIES

JACK DAVID & JON REDFERN

ECW

Canadian Cataloguing in Publication Data

Main entry under title:
Short short stories

ISBN 0-920763-98-7

1. Short stories. I. David, Jack, 1946-
II. Redfern, Jon.

PN6120.2.S56   823'.0108   C81-094602-5

The authors would like to thank Phyllis Bruce, Max David, Sharon David, Geoff Hancock, Robert Levinson, Gladys Neale, Sarah Norton, Chuck Redfern, and Chris Reibling.

"The Slump" by John Updike from *Museums and Women and Other Stories* is reprinted by permission of Alfred A. Knopf, Inc. "The Parrot" by Jacques Ferron, translated by Betty Bednarski, is reprinted by permission of House of Anansi Press. "My Life with R. H. Macy" by Shirley Jackson from *The Lottery* is reprinted by permission of Farrar, Straus & Giroux, Inc. "The Gunfighter" by Alden Nowlan from *Miracle at Indian River* © 1968 by Clarke, Irwin & Company Limited. Used by permission. "Keeping Fit" by Matt Cohen is reprinted by permission of the author. "The Collected Works of Billy the Kid" (excerpt) by Michael Ondaatje is reprinted by permission of House of Anansi Press. "Pierrette's Bumps" from *The Hockey Sweater and Other Stories*, by Roch Carrier, translated by Sheila Fischman, is reprinted by permission of House of Anansi Press. "When Greek Meets Greek" by Sam Selvon is reprinted by permission of the author. "A Room" by Doris Lessing is reprinted by kind permission of Curtis Brown on behalf of Doris Lessing. "A High Dive" by L. P. Hartley from *The Complete Short Stories of L. P. Hartley* is reprinted by permission of Hamish Hamilton Ltd. Copyright © 1973 the Executors of the Estate of the late L. P. Hartley. "Mary" by Edna O'Brien from *Mrs. Rinehart and Other Stories* is reprinted by permission of George Wiedenfeld & Nicholson Ltd. "The Kissing Man" by George Elliott from *the Kissing Man* is reprinted by permission of Macmillan of Canada, a division of Gage Publishing Ltd. "Up in Michigan" by Ernest Hemingway from *The Short Stories of Ernest Hemingway*. Copyright 1938 by Ernest Hemingway. Copyright renewed 1966 by Mary Hemingway. Reprinted with the permission of Charles Scribner's Sons. "6550" by Suzanne Jacob, translated by Donald Winkler, is reprinted by permission of the author. "The Turtle" by Robert Fones is reprinted by permission of the author. "Whole" by Steven Schrader is reprinted by permission of the author. "Snow" by Gwendolyn MacEwen is reprinted from *Noman* by permission of Oberon Press. "The Man Who Loved Flowers" by Stephen King copyright © 1977 by Montcalm Publishing Company, Inc. From the book *Night Shift* by Stephen King, copyright © 1978 by Stephen King. Reprinted by permission of Doubleday & Company, Inc. "Charles" by Shirley Jackson from *The Lottery* is reprinted by permission of Farrar, Straus & Giroux, Inc. "The Fourth Alarm" by John Cheever from *The Stories of John Cheever* is reprinted by permission of Alfred A. Knopf. Inc. "Bridal Suite" by Frederic Raphael from *Sleeps Six and Other Stories* is reprinted by permission of Jonathan Cape Ltd. "Giving Birth" (excerpt) by Margaret Atwood is reprinted by permission of the Canadian Publishers, McClelland and Stewart Limited, Toronto. "The World War I Los Angeles Airplane" by Richard Brautigan from *Revenge of the Lawn* is reprinted by permission of Simon and Schuster. "Sayin Good-bye to Tom" by Jonathan Strong from *Tike and Other Stories*. Copyright © 1969 by Jonathan Strong. "The Prodigal Parent" by Mavis Gallant is reprinted by permission of Georges Borchardt, Inc. "1912: The Bridge Beginning" by Wade Bell is reprinted by permission of the author. "Be Fruitful and Multiply" by Madeleine Ferron, translated by Sheila Watson, is reprinted by permission of the author. "The Use of Force" by William Carlos Williams from *The Farmer's Daughters*. Copyright 1938 by William Carlos Williams. Reprinted by permission of New Directions. "Heil!" by Randy Brown is reprinted by permission of the author. "The Blue Bouquet" by Octavio Paz, translated by Lysander Kemp, from *Eagle or Sun?* Copyright © 1976 by Octavio Paz. Reprinted by permission of New Directions. "The Autopsy" by Georg Heym, translated by Michael Hamburger, is reprinted by permission of the translator. "Mariana" by Fritz Leiber is reprinted by permission of Robert P. Mills. "Blackmail" by Fred Hoyle is reprinted by permission of the author. "The Handler" by Damon Knight is reprinted by permission of the author. "The Crime in the Attic" from *The Other Side of the Mirror* (El Grimorio) by Enrique Anderson Imbert. Authorized Translation and Introduction by Isabel Reade. Foreword by J. Cary Davis. Copyright © 1966 by Southern Illinois University Press. Reprinted by permission of Southern Illinois University Press. "The Elephant" by Slawomir Mrozek, translated by Konrad Syrop. Copyright © 1962 by Slawomir Mrozek. "Bug-Getter" by Reginald Bretnor is reprinted by permission of the author. "Continuity of Parks" by Julio Cortazár, translated by Paul Blackburn, from *The End of the Game and Other Stories* is reprinted by permission of Pantheon. "Steps" (excerpt) by Jerzy Kosinski from *Steps* is reprinted by permission of Random House. "A Storyteller's Shoptalk" by Raymond Carver is reprinted from *The New York Times Book Review*, February 15, 1981. © The New York Times Company. Used by permission.

SHORT SHORT PREFACE

◆

This anthology of short short fiction has been put together for two reasons—to introduce students to the art of concise prose writing and to make available a selection of stories that can be studied and discussed during a single class period. As teachers of English, we sought out stories that would both entertain students and teach them about the power and skill of good writing in a brief form. The authors whose works met these criteria represent not only Canada (French and English), the United States, and England but also Ireland, Germany, Poland, Trinidad, Mexico, Argentina, and Siberia.

The arrangement of the stories in sections is based on the controlling theme of personal relationships. Each section explores a type of personal encounter that most students have experienced or like to talk about. The title of the section indicates the kind of relationship explored in the stories. For instance, stories in the section titled "Parents, Partners, and Pals" deal with marriage, birth, father-and-daughter conflicts, and the making and breaking of youthful friendships. In the section "Lovers and Haters," the story writers use a variety of styles, from dreamy realism to a kind of poetic science fiction, to tell stories about love and hate.

We hope that teachers will use this book creatively, mixing and matching stories from each section in order to illustrate how a writer puts together a piece of fiction. We have also included a section of creative suggestions on how to use the stories herein, and an essay by Raymond Carver that explains some of the joys and pitfalls of being a short-story writer.

JACK DAVID   JON REDFERN

TABLE OF CONTENTS

PART ONE

LONERS AND ODDBALLS

PART TWO

LOVERS AND HATERS

PART THREE

PARENTS, PARTNERS, AND PALS

PART FOUR

THE USE OF FORCE

◆

PART FIVE

MIND-BOGGLERS

◆

◆

PART ONE
LONERS AND ODDBALLS

◆

1

JOHN UPDIKE (1932–) WAS BORN IN SHILLINGTON, PENNSYLVANIA. IN HIS NOVELS, SHORT STORIES, POETRY, AND ESSAYS, UPDIKE OFTEN USES WELL-KNOWN STORIES FROM GREEK MYTHOLOGY OR THE BIBLE. HIS BOOKS INCLUDE *RABBIT, RUN*, *COUPLES*, *RABBIT REDUX*, AND *THE COUP*.

THE SLUMP

John Updike

They say reflexes, the coach says reflexes, even the papers now are saying reflexes, but I don't think it's the reflexes so much—last night, as a gag to cheer me up, the wife walks into the bedroom wearing one of the kids' rubber gorilla masks and I was under the bed in six-tenths of a second, she had the stopwatch on me. It's that I can't see the ball the way I used to. It used to come floating up with all seven continents showing, and the pitcher's thumbprint, and a grass smooch or two, and the Spalding guarantee in ten-point sans-serif, and *whop!* I could feel the sweet wood with the bat still cocked. Now, I don't know, there's like a cloud around it, a sort of spiral vagueness, maybe the Van Allen belt, or maybe I lift my eye in the last second, planning how I'll round second base, or worrying which I do first, tip my cap or slap the third-base coach's hand. You can't see a blind spot, Kierkegaard says, but in there now, between when the ball leaves the bleacher background and I can hear it plop all fat and satisfied in the catcher's mitt, there's somehow just nothing, where there used to be a lot, everything in fact, because they're not keeping me around for my fielding, and already I see the afternoon tabloid has me down as trade bait.

The flutters don't come when they used to. It used to be, I'd back the convertible out of the garage and watch the electric eye put the door down again and drive in to the stadium, and at about the bridge turnoff I'd ease off grooving with the radio rock, and then on the lot there'd be the kids waiting to get a look and that would start the big butterflies, and when the attendant would take my car I'd want to shout *Stop, thief*, and walking down that long cement corridor I'd fantasize like I was going to the electric chair and the locker room was some dream after death, and I'd wonder why the suit fit, and how these really immortal guys, that I recognized from the bubble-gum cards I used to collect, knew my name. *They* knew *me*. And I'd go out and the stadium mumble would scoop at me and the grass seemed too precious to walk on, like emeralds, and by the time I got into the cage I couldn't remember if I batted left or right.

Now, hell, I move over the bridge singing along with the radio, and brush through the kids at just the right speed, not so fast I knock any of them down, and the attendant knows his Labor Day tip is coming, and we wink, and in the batting cage I own the place, and take my cuts, and pop five or six into the bullpen as easy as dropping dimes down a sewer. But when the scoreboard lights up, and I take those two steps up from the dugout, the biggest two steps in a ballplayer's life, and kneel in the circle, giving the crowd the old hawk profile, where once the flutters would ease off, now they dig down and begin.

They say I'm not hungry, but I still feel hungry, only now it's a kind of panic hungry, and that's not the right kind. Ever watch one of your little kids try to catch a ball? He gets so excited with the idea he's going to catch it he shuts his eyes. That's me now. I walk up to the plate, having come all this way—a lot of hotels, a lot of shagging—and my eyes feel shut. And I stand up there trying to push my eyeballs through my eyelids, and my retinas register maybe a little green, and the black patch of some nuns in far left field. That's panic hungry.

Kierkegaard called it dread. It queers the works.

My wife comes at me without the gorilla mask and when in the old days, *whop!*, now she slides by with a hurt expression and a flicker of gray above her temple. I go out and ride the power mower and I've already done it so often the lawn is brown. The kids get me out of bed for a little fungo and it scares me to see them trying, busting their lungs, all that shagging ahead of them. In Florida—we used to love it in Florida, the smell of citrus and marlin, the flat pink sections where the old people drift around smiling with transistor plugs in their ears—we lie on the beach after a workout and the sun seems a high fly I'm going to lose and the waves keep coming like they've been doing for a billion years, up to the plate, up to the plate. Kierkegaard probably has the clue, somewhere in there, but I picked up *Concluding Unscientific Postscript* the other day and I couldn't see the print, that is, I could see the lines, but there wasn't anything on them, like the rows of deep seats in the shade of the second deck on a Thursday afternoon, just a single ice-cream vendor sitting there, nobody around to sell to, a speck of white in all that shade, old Søren Sock himself, keeping his goods cool.

I think maybe if I got beaned. That's probably what the wife is hinting at with the gorilla mask. A change of pace, like the time DiMaggio broke his slump by Topping's telling him to go to a night club and get plastered. I've stopped ducking, but the trouble is, if you're not hitting, they don't brush you back. On me, they've stopped trying for even the corners; they put it right down the pike. I can see it in his evil eye as he takes the sign and rears back, I can hear the catcher snicker, and for a second of reflex there I can see it like it used to be, continents and cities and every green tree distinct as a stitch, and the hickory sweetens in my hands, and I feel the good old sure hunger. Then something happens. It blurs, skips, fades, I don't know. It's not caring enough, is what it probably is, it's knowing that none of it—the stadium, the averages—is really there, just *you* are there, and it's not enough.

JACQUES FERRON
(1921–   ) WAS BORN IN
LOUISVILLE, QUEBEC.
HIS SHORT FICTION AND
PLAYS COMBINE
FANTASY AND REALISM,
AND OFTEN SATIRIZE
THE SMALL-TOWN LIFE
OF QUEBEC. HIS FIRST
COLLECTION OF SHORT
STORIES, *CONTES DU
PAYS INCERTAIN,* WON
THE
GOVERNOR-GENERAL'S
AWARD IN 1962. HIS
NOVEL, *DR. COTNOIR,*
WAS TRANSLATED INTO
ENGLISH IN 1973.

THE PARROT

Jacques Ferron

Translated by Betty Bednarski

If she had been vulgar, coarse, fleshy, it might not have been so surprising, but she was, on the contrary, a very prim and proper lady, bony to say the least. What, then, could have possessed her to show her behind?

Her nephew appeared in my office, embarrassed, unsure how to go about telling me the awful truth.

"The fact is, doctor, my Aunt Donatienne has been behaving very strangely."

And he had come to ask for my help in getting her into a mental hospital. I wasn't surprised: it's the fashion now to shut people up. Faced with an undesirable who's not a criminal, we simply say he's sick, and he can be imprisoned without trial. In this respect medicine is a most useful institution, a branch of the law. Doctors themselves are generally well-fitted for their role; they make excellent jailers. All they have to learn now is the executioner's trade.

"But is she actually mad, this aunt of yours?" I asked the nephew.

"Oh yes, doctor."

"In what way?"

That he could not tell me. He asked me to come with him. I would see for myself in what way. So we set out together. The aunt lived at the rural end of Coteau-Rouge.

"Stop here," said my companion suddenly.

We stopped near a signpost that said, "Rue Sainte-Olive". The sign would have gladdened the heart of any nominalist philosopher: there was no street, only two or three houses in the middle of a field. The nephew pointed to one of them.

"There it is," he said.

"But that's Monsieur Comtois' house!"

"You're right," he replied. "It is."

And with a sheepish look in my direction he asked how it was I knew. I'd visited this Monsieur Comtois the year before. I remembered him well. A little old boy with whiskers in his ears, a nose chock full of crude jokes and cheeky as a monkey, who lived with his daughter and a parrot. The daughter was the kind of wised-up bird who knows her stuff, even though she's none too bright, the kind they call a floozy. It was rather surprising that she should have stayed with her daddy. As for the parrot, he hadn't made too good an impression on me either.

"A fine parrot you have there," I'd said to Monsieur Comtois. As if in response to my words, the bird had begun to flutter its wings.

"He's a vain little fellow," the old man had replied.

"Does he talk?"

"No, but he's got something he'd like to show you."

"What's that?" I asked.

I could have saved myself the trouble. My curiosity had been well received. They lost no time in satisfying it.

"Coco," said the daughter, "would you like to show the doctor what a smart boy you are?"

Coco having indicated that he would (it was obvious from his fluttering), she continued: "Go on, Coco, show him your bum. Show the nice doctor your bum."

And, painstakingly, the bird had shown it.

Once the ceremony was over, the homage paid, I'd busied myself with old Comtois, who was having an attack of colic. The case had baffled me. I'd nevertheless comforted him as best I could. That's the way I practise. I'm ruthlessly optimistic. The old boy had never called me again. So I'd assumed he was cured.

"How's Monsieur Comtois these days?" I inquired.

"Dead," my companion answered flatly.

That's the trouble with optimism: you can't keep it up for long. Even though I'd not ruled out the possibility of his dying, I'd still not foreseen that he'd lose his cheekiness so soon. "He must have fallen into the hands of a pessimistic doctor," I thought.

We were almost at the house. The nephew explained that Comtois had been his Aunt Donatienne's brother.

"But," he added, obviously embarrassed, "he was not the father of his daughter."

After his death the orphan had been advised to find herself another daddy, and Aunt Donatienne had taken over the inheritance. At first she seemed happy, then the parrot died . . . We were there.

"Come in, doctor," said the nephew.

I went in first. A little old lady, modestly attired, was sitting on the edge of a chair in the attitude of a novice awaiting her bishop. The awkwardness of the position seemed to suit her. She was reading with an air of quiet contentment. We had been standing inside for some time before she deigned to acknowledge our presence. Affecting surprise, she got hurriedly to her feet. I begged her to sit down again, which she did, most readily. The house was spotless. There was a certain elegance about the place, rare in the rural end of Coteau-Rouge, and I took it to be an innovation, since I didn't recall having been aware of it in the days when old Comtois had occupied the premises with his floozy.

The old lady had closed her missal. We embarked on a conversation that was polite, refined, flowery, but dreadfully trite — as trite as paper flowers for a side altar. As soon as I ventured anything less insipid, she would take fright, and her answers would become evasive. Embarrassed myself, I would take refuge again in the pious artificiality that she found fitting. When the time came for me to leave, I had discovered nothing. In fact I was quite captivated by this aunt and could find only the most complimentary things to say about her to her nephew, as he led me away.

"Well, she's refined all right, is Aunt Donatienne," the nephew admitted. "But there's a reason for that. She worked for thirty years with her elder sister in the millinery business — making feathered hats for Society ladies. There's no trade like it for giving you airs. Then her sister died and she went into a convent. Terribly posh, shiniest floors you've ever seen: you needed the grace of God to walk around in the place."

"Why didn't she stay there?"

"At the convent? That's simple: at night she never slept. She wandered around the dormitories like a ghost. Or if there was a nun or a boarder she particularly fancied she'd go sit on the edge of her bed and watch over her while she slept. She imagined she was some kind of guardian angel."

"She'd let herself get too refined."

"Perhaps so. But the trouble was she had everyone scared to death. In the end they threw her out. I took her in. Then, when her brother died, she came to live here."

"I'm beginning to understand," I said.

The nephew gave me a searching look. He had let himself get carried away on the subject of his aunt's fine manners, manners of which he was proud, but that did not mean he'd forgotten his plan, which was to get her into a mental hospital. Worried, he asked me, "You do think she's mad, don't you, doctor?"

"Peculiar, perhaps. Affected, certainly. But she's not mad. If that were madness we'd have to clear out the convents and the academies and lock up all the poetesses in Canada and all the nuns on earth."

He seemed surprised at my lack of discernment.

"But," he objected, "are the nuns and poetesses of Canada in the habit of showing their behinds to passers by?"

"To my knowledge, Aunt Donatienne has not shown me hers," I retorted, piqued.

Now it was my turn to scrutinize him. He seemed sure of himself. Then I remembered the parrot.

"Good God, it can't be true."

It was true. Aunt Donatienne had not only inherited the house, but the parrot too. At first she had tried to teach him to pray: "Coco, say, 'The Lord's name be praised!'"

She was wasting her time. Coco had continued to show his behind. The old lady had had to accept it. After a while she had begun to enjoy it. The bird's fluttering excited her. From then on she was forever telling him:

"Coco, show me your bum."

Until in the end poor Coco had died of it. After that she had taken to showing her own. And in no time word had got round. She couldn't go out now without a band of children following at her heels. The more the children squealed, the more excited she got, and the more she showed them what they wanted to see. At night the local perverts prowled around outside the little house, terrorizing the lady who had once taken herself for a guardian angel.

We had stopped to talk outside the front door. It was a sunny afternoon. The

9

sunlight was reflected in the window panes. A cloud passed overhead. Before leaving, I glanced back at the window. I saw something white. It was Aunt Donatienne. It was this very prim and proper lady showing us her poor, frilly behind.

SHIRLEY JACKSON
(1919 – 65) WAS BORN IN
SAN FRANCISCO,
CALIFORNIA. HER
STORIES ARE NOTED
FOR THEIR
ATMOSPHERE OF
GOTHIC HORROR AND
BROODING FANTASY.
HER BOOKS INCLUDE
THE LOTTERY AND
SUCH MACABRE WORKS
AS *THE HAUNTING OF
HILL HOUSE* AND *THE
BIRD'S NEST.*

MY LIFE
WITH
R. H. MACY

Shirley Jackson

And the first thing they did was segregate me. They segregated me from the only person in the place I had even a
speaking acquaintance with; that was a girl I had met going
down the hall who said to me: "Are you as scared as I am?" And
when I said, "Yes," she said, "I'm in lingerie, what are you in?" and
I thought for a while and then said, "Spun glass," which was as
good an answer as I could think of, and she said, "Oh. Well, I'll meet
you here in a sec." And she went away and was segregated and I
never saw her again.

Then they kept calling my name and I kept trotting over to wherever they
called it and they would say ("They" all this time being startlingly beautiful
young women in tailored suits and with short-clipped hair), "Go with Miss
Cooper, here. She'll tell you what to do." All the women I met my first day were
named Miss Cooper. And Miss Cooper would say to me: "What are you in?" and I
had learned by that time to say, "Books," and she would say, "Oh, well, then, you
belong with Miss Cooper here," and then she would call "Miss Cooper?" and
another young woman would come and the first one would say, "13-3138 here
belongs with you," and Miss Cooper would say, "What is she in?" and Miss
Cooper would answer, "Books," and I would go away and be segregated again.

Then they taught me. They finally got me segregated into a classroom, and I
sat there for a while all by myself (that's how far segregated I was) and then a
few other girls came in, all wearing tailored suits (I was wearing a red velvet
afternoon frock) and we sat down and they taught us. They gave us each a big
book with R. H. Macy written on it, and inside this book were pads of little
sheets saying (from left to right): "Comp. keep for ref. cust. d.a. no. or c.t. no.

salesbook no. salescheck no. clerk no. dept. date M." After M there was a long line for Mr. or Mrs. and the name, and then it began again with "No. item. class. at price. total." And down at the bottom was written ORIGINAL and then again, "Comp. keep for ref.," and "Paste yellow gift stamp here." I read all this very carefully. Pretty soon a Miss Cooper came, who talked for a little while on the advantages we had in working at Macy's, and she talked about the salesbooks, which it seems came apart into a sort of road map and carbons and things. I listened for a while, and when Miss Cooper wanted us to write on the little pieces of paper, I copied from the girl next to me. That was training.

Finally someone said we were going on the floor, and we descended from the sixteenth floor to the first. We were in groups of six by then, all following Miss Cooper doggedly and wearing little tags saying BOOK INFORMATION. I never did find out what that meant. Miss Cooper said I had to work on the special sale counter, and showed me a little book called *The Stage-Struck Seal*, which it seemed I would be selling. I had gotten about halfway through it before she came back to tell me I had to stay with my unit.

I enjoyed meeting the time clock, and spent a pleasant half-hour punching various cards standing around, and then someone came in and said I couldn't punch the clock with my hat on. So I had to leave, bowing timidly at the time clock and its prophet, and I went and found out my locker number, which was 1773, and my time-clock number, which was 712, and my cash-box number, which was 1336, and my cash-register number, which was 253, and my cash-register-drawer number, which was K, and my cash-register-drawer-key number, which was 872, and my department number, which was 13. I wrote all these numbers down. And that was my first day.

My second day was better. I was officially on the floor. I stood in a corner of a counter, with one hand possessively on *The Stage-Struck Seal*, waiting for customers. The counter head was named 13-2246, and she was very kind to me. She sent me to lunch three times, because she got me confused with 13-6454 and 13-3141. It was after lunch that a customer came. She came over and took one of my stage-struck seals, and said "How much is this?" I opened my mouth and the customer said "I have a D.A. and I will have this sent to my aunt in Ohio. Part of that D.A. I will pay for with a book dividend of 32 cents, and the rest of course will be on my account. Is this book price-fixed?" That's as near as I can remember what she said. I smiled confidently, and said "Certainly; will you wait just one moment?" I found a little piece of paper in a drawer under the counter: it had "Duplicate Triplicate" printed across the front in big letters. I took down the customer's name and address, her aunt's name and address, and wrote carefully across the front of the duplicate triplicate "1 Stg. Strk. Sl." Then I smiled at the customer again and said carelessly: "That will be seventy-five cents." She said "But I have a D.A." I told her that all D.A.'s were suspended for the Christmas rush, and she gave me seventy-five cents, which I kept. Then I rang up a "No Sale" on the cash register and I tore up the duplicate triplicate because I didn't know what else to do with it.

Later on another customer came and said "Where would I find a copy of Ann Rutherford Gwynn's *He Came Like Thunder*?" and I said "In medical books, right across the way," but 13-2246 came and said "That's philosophy, isn't it?" and the customer said it was, and 13-2246 said "Right down this aisle, in dictionaries." The customer went away, and I said to 13-2246 that her guess was as good as mine, anyway, and she stared at me and explained that philosophy, social sciences and Bertrand Russell were all kept in dictionaries.

14

So far I haven't been back to Macy's for my third day, because that night when I started to leave the store, I fell down the stairs and tore my stockings and the doorman said that if I went to my department head Macy's would give me a new pair of stockings and I went back and I found Miss Cooper and she said, "Go to the adjuster on the seventh floor and give him this," and she handed me a little slip of pink paper and on the bottom of it was printed "Comp. keep for ref. cust. d.a. no. or c.t. no. salesbook no. salescheck no. clerk no. dept. date M." And after M, instead of a name, she had written 13-3138. I took the little pink slip and threw it away and went up to the fourth floor and bought myself a pair of stockings for $.69 and then I came down and went out the customers' entrance.

I wrote Macy's a long letter, and I signed it with all my numbers added together and divided by 11,700, which is the number of employees in Macy's. I wonder if they miss me.

ALDEN NOWLAN (1933–)
IS A NATIVE OF NOVA
SCOTIA WHO IS BEST
KNOWN FOR HIS POETRY
ABOUT THE RURAL
TOWNSFOLK OF THE
MARITIMES. HIS
COLLECTION OF SHORT
STORIES, *MIRACLE AT
INDIAN RIVER*, DEALS
WITH THE DREAMS AND
FAILURES OF
SMALL-TOWN LIFE. HIS
FIRST NOVEL, *VARIOUS
PERSONS NAMED
KEVIN O'BRIEN*, CAME
OUT IN 1973.

THE GUNFIGHTER

Alden Nowlan

I come out of the Lord Wellington Hotel, where I have interviewed a famous politician who told me that the Jews were out to get him, but that he would sue *The Clarion* if I quoted him. "Those fellows are still trying to rub the blood off their hands," the politician had said. "But I'm not dead yet. I'm going to save this Canada of ours despite the Jews and the Frenchmen. By the way, did you ever hear why the States has the Darkies and Canada has the Frenchmen?" Here the honourable gentleman paused and smiled benignly. "It's because the States had first choice." racist

It is about ten o'clock on a crisp December night and the square is a kaleidoscope of Christmas lights. In Princess Park a spotlight illuminates Samuel de Champlain, his marble hand outstretched toward Europe, his back turned on North America. As I walk past the Monte Carlo Restaurant, the glass door opens and a swarm of laughing adolescents rushes by me. For a moment the air smells of french fries, hamburgers and pizzas. In the window of the Air Canada ticket office, there are signs urging me to vacation in Bermuda, Jamaica and Spain.

"Hey, Kevin! Kevin O'Brien!"

The Wichita Kid is hailing me from across the street. He stands in front of Tony's Mag and Fag Shop, a baroque figure in a black gaucho hat laced under his chin, a black and red neckerchief, an imitation buckskin jacket, black levis and high-heeled boots. Two Buntline Specials hang low on his hips, their imitation-silver-plated holsters strapped to his thighs.

I cross the street, dodging cars, almost losing my footing on a patch of ice.

"Hello, Wichita. I haven't seen you for a thousand years. What's new with the fastest gun east of Montreal?"

[Wichita looks old at nineteen, and will look young at fifty.] He has felt joy and sadness, but neither has left its mark on his face.] His lips are full, his eyes blue-grey, his cheeks red from the cold.

He punches my shoulder and laughs.

"Been away," he says. "Been out in Missouri. You know. Across the wide Missouri." He laughs again. Passers-by glance our way and grin. Several of them nod or wave to Wichita, who is given the mock-obeisance the ancients gave their sacrificial kings. One day, perhaps, the Mayor will proclaim a holiday, and Wichita, smiling happily, will be offered up to the waning moon or the setting sun.

"Missouri, eh? What have you been doing out there?" Tony's show window contains cigars twelve inches long, pepper-flavoured chewing gum, trick beer glasses that won't pour, "physical culture" magazines, the covers of which show boys naked except for jockstraps. I think of the Bizarro World in one of my son's comic books, in which everything on earth is reversed, a world in which, I suppose, men are born old and become younger and younger until at last they die of youth.

Wichita's mouth is close to my ear. "I been riding with Dingus and Buck," he confides.

"Dingus and Buck. Oh, I remember. Those were their nicknames. Jesse and Frank James."

"Sure. Dingus and Frank. I was with 'em at Liberty and Lexington and Richmond—"

"And I suppose you helped rob the Gallatin bank and the Glendale train. Isn't that what the song says?

Oh, it was Jess and Frank
Who robbed the Gallatin bank,
Held up the Glendale train;
With the agent on his knees,
He delivered up the keys
To those outlaws, Frank and Jesse James."

"Don't talk crazy," Wichita says, "the Gallatin robbery hasn't happened yet. It won't happen until 1869. Don't you even know what year this is? This is only 1867."

"I guess I didn't stop to think, Wichita. Sorry."

The televised head and shoulders of the famous politician appear in the window of Bill's TV Sales and Service. He is smiling like a madman enjoying a secret joke: it is a Vincent Price kind of smile. I can't hear him through the plate glass but earlier in the hotel he gave me an advance copy of his speech, so I know he is saying that this Canada of ours is a mosaic and not a melting pot and that all men of goodwill must put their shoulders to the wheel to create a country in which brotherhood is not just a word but a way of life.

"What's that you say, Wichita? I'm sorry. I'm afraid I wasn't listening."

"I said, do you know how many notches I have on my sixguns now?"

"I haven't any idea, Wichita. Tell me."

"Make a guess."

"No, really, I couldn't. Tell me."

"You won't believe me."

"I'll believe almost anything, Wichita. Come on, tell me."

"Forty-two!"

"Forty-two."

18

"Yep. Billy the Kid, he only had twenty-one. I've gunned down more men than Billy the Kid, Wild Bill Hickok, Jesse James and John Wesley Harden put together."

Gunfighters *Hero's* *rob trains* *represent freedom*

"By Gad, sir, I do admire you."

"You making fun of me or something?"

"I wouldn't think of it, Wichita." *outcast but at same time cannot take place* *situation*

"Here. Look." He removes his pistols from their holsters and shows me their butts. I don't count the notches, but there are many of them, chipped into the plastic. Suddenly I feel as sad and guilty as I felt once after I absent-mindedly pushed in front of an old woman waiting at the check-out counter in a supermarket and she whimpered "I'm sorry," she was that used to begging forgiveness. At that moment I felt as if I were responsible for creating the old woman who apologized when other people were rude to her. *IRONIC because he pushed her.*

Now I feel that I have created Wichita. *insecure, low self-esteem* *victim* *mentality* *level of abuse*

"I'd better be on my way," I tell him. "Do you have a place to sleep? It's getting colder all the time." I rub my ears and clap my hands together, as though to convince him.

"I don't sleep much," he says. "Later, when everybody goes home, maybe I'll ride my horse down Trafalgar Street. I do that, sometimes, when I feel like it."

"Sure, Wichita, sure. But you'd better take this anyway." I press a dollar bill into his hand. "Put that in your pocket where you won't lose it. It will buy you some soup and coffee, or maybe a hot sandwich, something hot anyway." I put two quarters in his other hand. "Put those in your other pocket, and don't lose them, either. They'll pay for a bed at the Salvation Army. Do you understand me, Wichita?"

On second thought, I take the money from his hands and put it in the pockets of his jacket. "Don't forget where it is, Wichita. Okay?"

He grabs the sleeve of my topcoat.

"Ghosts," he says, "Ghosts!"

"Huh?"

"I keep seeing the ghosts of the men I've killed. And the worst part of it is they don't know that they're dead. That fellow that went past a second ago, did you see him? The guy in the UNB jacket—"

"Easy now, Kid. Easy now."

"—Young punk with a smirk on his kisser. Smirking little bastard. I killed him a week ago, and he doesn't know. What do you think of that, huh? What do you think of that?"

"Maybe it's better that way, Kid. What they don't know won't hurt them."

He releases my arm, steps back, draws his sixguns and shoots. One pistol is pointed at my head, the other at my belly. At this distance, he can't miss. *Bang! Bang!* He empties both guns. *Pressure gets on he can just say release*

I laugh, nervously. "Well, so long, Kid. I'll be seeing you around. Don't forget about your money." I turn away and walk rapidly down the street toward the parking lot. *keeps himself sane.*

Wichita screams after me. "You see what I mean?" he yells. "You see what I mean?"

what society does with psychopath.

ANGER

Child acting out frustration. (anger)
pride ⇒ any adult know what they do wrong.

MATT COHEN (1942–)
WAS BORN IN KINGSTON,
ONTARIO. COHEN
OFTEN MIXES THE
SURREAL AND THE
EVERYDAY IN HIS
FICTION. HIS
BEST-KNOWN BOOK OF
SHORT STORIES,
*COLUMBUS AND THE
FAT LADY AND OTHER
STORIES*, APPEARED IN
1972. HIS NOVELS
INCLUDE *THE
DISINHERITED, THE
SWEET SECOND
SUMMER OF KITTY
MALONE*, AND
*FLOWERS OF
DARKNESS*. "KEEPING
FIT" WAS COHEN'S FIRST
PUBLISHED SHORT
STORY.

KEEPING FIT

Matt Cohen

When he had started training it was always the breath that went first. That didn't surprise him; he knew that at 32 and with ten years of inactivity behind him it would take a long time. But after a couple of weeks, when he had worked up to doing a slow mile and had quit smoking, it became his legs and ankles. It wasn't for several months, when he was running six and seven miles at a stretch, that his feet began to bother him. It was funny; he had never thought of himself as having particularly good feet but somehow he had never encountered the problem of blisters and sores. But by the time he was up to ten miles the pain was always and exclusively in his feet. No matter what he did—he had tried all sorts of salves—even an antibiotic a couple of times—there didn't seem to be any way he could prevent the blistering. He remembered the difficulty of getting into condition too well to stop running for a couple of weeks to let his feet heal so he just bandaged them up and did his best to ignore them. If he was running smoothly, and lately he was always running smoothly, it took at least six miles for the bandages to work themselves off. After the first irritation of squashing them to a more comfortable place in his shoes it was two or three miles until they really started to hurt. He would run another fifteen minutes thinking of almost nothing but his feet and feeling the separateness of each sharp pain. Finally the hurt would melt together and he would run until he had to stop. The bandages were coming off now, he had felt the first twitch at the bottom of the hill; once they started they worked loose pretty fast. He ran easily along the shoulder of the level stretch of highway. The cars didn't bother him and he had long ago quit caring about people staring at him. Actually, he liked running along level ground even better than downhill and had, for a while, considered moving west. There was a feeling of continuous motion that, after the first few minutes, he would slowly sink into. When he had first been able to do ten miles he had thought about giving up his project and becoming a long-distance runner. He went out one night to a track club; it was summer and they practiced in the evening. But, not really to his surprise, he found running with other people distracting. So he never went back and instead kept running on the streets and by the highway. He was halfway at least through the painful part now. It didn't seem as bad today though he wasn't sure whether he liked that or not. As usual he couldn't think very clearly when he ran. In fact he could hardly think at all. That was one of the things that had attracted him to it. He thought a lot afterwards, about what he was doing and about other things. But when he ran he thought of nothing and was only barely conscious of his own movements and, of course, the cycle of his foot blisters. Going around a bend of the highway there was a last brief moment of sharp pain and then it all diffused. He loped along for another couple of hundred yards and turned onto a dirt road. It extended at least ten miles, according to the map, and he knew that would be far enough. He kept running. The motion had taken him over. After a while, he didn't know how long, he noticed he was slowing down and speeded up a little before settling into his customary rhythm. He had wanted it to be like that, smooth and easy, an imperceptible transition, and when they found him the next day they thought he had collapsed in mid-stride.

MICHAEL ONDAATJE (1943–) WAS BORN IN CEYLON (NOW CALLED SRI LANKA) AND ATTENDED SCHOOLS IN ENGLAND AND CANADA. HE IS NOW TEACHING AT YORK UNIVERSITY IN TORONTO, ONTARIO. ALTHOUGH HE IS BEST KNOWN AS A POET, HIS EXPERIMENTAL FICTION HAS WON SEVERAL AWARDS. THIS EXCERPT IS TAKEN FROM *THE COLLECTED WORKS OF BILLY THE KID*, WHICH WON A GOVERNOR-GENERAL'S AWARD IN 1970.

THE COLLECTED WORKS OF BILLY THE KID
(excerpt)

Michael Ondaatje

The barn I stayed in for a week then was at the edge of a farm and had been deserted it seemed for several years, though built of stone and good wood. The cold dark grey of the place made my eyes become used to soft light and I burned out my fever there. It was twenty yards long, about ten yards wide. Above me was another similar sized room but the floors were unsafe for me to walk on. However I heard birds and the odd animal scrape their feet, the rotten wood magnifying the sound so they entered my dreams and nightmares.

But it was the colour and light of the place that made me stay there, not my fever. It became a calm week. It was the colour and the light. The colour a grey with remnants of brown — for instance those rust brown pipes and metal objects that before had held bridles or pails, that slid to machine uses; the thirty or so grey cans in one corner of the room, their ellipses, from where I sat, setting up patterns in the dark.

When I had arrived I opened two windows and a door and the sun poured blocks and angles in, lighting up the floor's skin of feathers and dust and old grain. The windows looked out onto fields and plants grew at the door, me killing them gradually with my urine. Wind came in wet and brought in birds who flew to the other end of the room to get their aim to fly out again. An old tap hung from the roof, the same colour as the walls, so once I knocked myself out on it.

For that week then I made a bed of the table there and lay out my fever, whatever it was. I began to block my mind of all thought. Just sensed the room and learnt what my body could do, what it could survive, what colours it liked best, what songs I sang best. There were animals who did not move out and accepted me as a larger breed. I ate the old grain with them, drank from a constant puddle about twenty yards away from the barn. I saw no human and heard no human voice, learned to squat the best way when shitting, used leaves for wiping, never ate flesh or touched another animal's flesh, never entered his boundary. We were all aware and allowed each other. The fly who sat on my arm, after his inquiry, just went away, ate his disease and kept it in him. When I walked I avoided the cobwebs who had places to grow to, who had stories to finish. The flies caught in those acrobat nets were the only murder I saw.

And in the barn next to us there was another granary, separated by just a thick wood door. In it a hundred or so rats, thick rats, eating and eating the foot deep pile of grain abandoned now and fermenting so that at the end of my week, after a heavy rain storm burst the power in those seeds and brought drunkenness into the minds of those rats, they abandoned the sanity of eating the food before them and turned on each other and grotesque and awkwardly because of their size they went for each other's eyes and ribs so the yellow stomachs slid out and they came through that door and killed a chipmunk—about ten of them onto that one striped thing and the ten eating each other before they realised the chipmunk was long gone so that I, sitting on the open window with its thick sill where they couldn't reach me, filled my gun and fired again and again into their slow wheel across the room at each boommm, and reloaded and fired again and again till I went through the whole bag of bullet supplies—the noise breaking out the seal of silence in my ears, the smoke sucked out of the window as it emerged from my fist and the long twenty yard space between me and them empty but for the floating bullet lonely as an emissary across and between the wooden posts that never returned, so the rats continued to wheel and stop in the silences and eat each other, some even the bullet. Till my hand was black and the gun was hot and no other animal of any kind remained in that room but for the boy in the blue shirt sitting there coughing at the dust, rubbing the sweat of his upper lip with his left forearm.

ROCH CARRIER (1937–)
WAS BORN IN THE
BEAUCE REGION OF
QUEBEC, WHERE MANY
OF HIS STORIES ARE
SET. HE HAS WRITTEN
POEMS, SHORT STORIES,
AND PLAYS. CARRIER'S
WORK EXAMINES THE
RELIGIOUS, SOCIAL,
AND POLITICAL
CONCERNS OF THE
QUÉBÉCOIS IN SUCH
WORKS AS *LA GUERRE,
YES SIR!* AND *IS IT THE
SUN, PHILIBERT?*

PIERRETTE'S BUMPS

Roch Carrier

Translated by Sheila Fischman

Ever since we'd started school Pierrette was the tallest girl in our class, the one who sat in the last row at the back, the one who was always last when we marched through the village in order of height, accompanied by two nuns as the wind tried to pull away their veils. Pierrette was a quiet girl; she didn't really attract our attention except when, in a sentence during reading or an example in grammar, the word 'big' appeared; then all heads would turn in her direction and the classroom would be filled with noisy chortling; Pierrette would blush and be silent. Aside from that, Pierrette was like the rest of us, just another student; and that was why I wondered, when Pierrette walked by, why the big boys would stop yelling, put down their ball and stop to look at her.

One evening the men from the village were sitting with my father on the wooden gallery. Words rose in the air with the smoke from their pipes, words as dark as the night that was drawing near. They talked about how life was going badly in the world. But they declared they were happy there was a leader like Duplessis to protect Quebec. I listened, a child in their midst, fascinated by all that these men knew.

'I'm scared about the future,' said one of them. 'Duplessis won't be around forever, like the good Lord. And what'll happen to us when we haven't got Duplessis any more?'

Suddenly they were silent. They stopped smoking. Pierrette was walking along the sidewalk. Not talking, not smoking, they examined her. My father too.

'Watch out, Pierrette,' one of the men called, 'you're gonna lose them.'

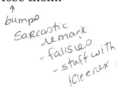

bumps
Sarcastic
remark
- falisies
- stuff with
Kleenex.

The others guffawed and slapped their thighs with their big workers' hands, bent over and shaken by their laughter. Pierrette walked faster, to escape.

'Papa,' I asked, 'what's Pierrette going to lose?'

Hearing me, the men were paralysed, as though struck by lightning.

'This is men's talk,' my father stammered, blushing.

The others, coming to his rescue, began to explain why it was that without Duplessis, 'they'd've never got electricity in the stables.'

I left the group of men. Just what was Pierrette going to lose? I was far more obsessed by this question than by the future of Quebec or the politics of Duplessis. It prevented me from sleeping.

In the schoolyard the next day, I approached the territory reserved by the big boys for playing ball. A few minutes later, Pierrette appeared. The big boys broke off their game as though the ball had become a heavy stone. Their eyes followed Pierrette as though she were the Pope. It was time to take action.

'Watch out, Pierrette,' I shouted, 'you're gonna lose them.'

Pierrette fled, taking refuge in the school. One of the big boys picked up the ball and said to me majestically:

'Don't get in a sweat, kid, they won't fall off, they're fastened on good and solid. I checked myself.'

The ball began to fly from one boy to the other, joyously, amid bursts of laughter. I decided then to laugh louder than all the big boys. But I still didn't know what it was that Pierrette was going to lose, and what was so firmly fastened on.

For days my glance followed Pierrette; I invented all sorts of tricks to uncover her secret. I spied on her from behind an open book, I brought a little mirror that I used so I could see behind me, I hid under the stairs Pierrette would walk down. But Pierrette still looked as she always did, timid, plump, blushing and the biggest girl in our class. The big boys could have explained to me but I didn't dare display my ignorance, I was so afraid of their mockery.

One morning, to celebrate a religious holiday, our whole class was taken to the church. All in a row, by order of height, we went to take Communion. But scarcely had we returned to school when the nun curtly ordered Pierrette to stand up. Blushing, Pierrette obeyed.

'Instead of displaying such languorous, sensual postures in front of the men in our parish,' the indignant nun roared, 'you'd be better off praying to God, Pierrette, to chase the evil thoughts from your possessed body. When a person has such provocative bumps on her body it's because the Devil's within you.'

Pierrette's face became even redder, then it suddenly turned white; she swayed and crumpled to the floor.

'You see,' said the nun, 'the Devil is leaving her body.'

When I approached Pierrette, who had fallen to the yellow floor when she fainted, I didn't see the Devil but I noticed what I'd never noticed before: Pierrette's chest was puffed out just like a real woman's. But why couldn't the big boys go on playing ball when they saw her?

I hesitated for a long time before confiding in my friend Lapin.

'Pierrette fainted today because the Devil put bumps on her body. Two big bumps, right here!'

'Come on!' said Lapin, 'it wasn't the Devil that did that.'

My friend Lapin was doubly superior to me: he was older and his father worked in the office of Duplessis' government in Quebec. I understood what his profession was when, after school, behind the big rock we used as a secret hiding place, my friend Lapin opened a paper bag as I watched him.

'This comes from my father's office.'

He took out a dozen magazines that had nothing but photographs of girls on every page, girls with no clothes on; and all of them were possessed by the Devil because they had bumps! Bigger bumps than Pierrette. The magazines burned my hands like fire, but I was hungry to learn! I wanted to know! On every page I turned I could feel the sea of ignorance retreating. At every picture my body ceased to be that of a child and I became a man.

'These magazines come from the United States,' said Lapin.

'I'd like that, to live in the United States,' I said, slowly turning the pages.

I discovered that the United States was a truly amazing country because they knew how to print such beautiful magazines, while in Quebec the newspapers only knew how to take pictures of Cardinal Villeneuve or Maurice Duplessis in his old hat.

'In the United States,' Lapin explained, 'the streets are full of girls like that!'

'There can't be many Catholics in that country,' I said.

'In the Protestant religion there's no such thing as sin.'

As I couldn't leave for the United States immediately to become a Protestant, I went back to school the next day as usual. That morning, I played ball with the others. When Pierrette came into the schoolyard I put the ball on the ground and watched her go past with the same expression in my eyes as the big boys.

SAM SELVON (1923-)
WAS BORN IN TRINIDAD.
SELVON IS BEST KNOWN
FOR HIS NOVELS ABOUT
CARIBBEAN
IMMIGRANTS LIVING IN
ENGLAND. HIS BOOKS
INCLUDE *THE LONELY
LONDONERS, THE
HOUSING LARK,* AND
WAYS OF SUNLIGHT.

WHEN GREEK
MEETS GREEK

Sam Selvon

One morning Ramkilawansingh (after this, we calling this man Ram) was making a study of the notice-boards along Westbourne Grove what does advertise rooms to let. Every now and then he writing down an address or a telephone number, though most of the time his eyes colliding up with *No Colours, Please,* or *Sorry, No Kolors.*

"Red, white and blue, all out but you," Ram was humming a little ditty what children say when they playing whoop. Just as he get down by Bradley's Corner he met Fraser.

"You look like a man who looking for a place to live," Fraser say.

"You look like a man who could tell me the right place to go," Ram say.

"You try down by Ladbroke Grove?" Fraser ask.

"I don't want to go down in that criminal area," Ram say, "at least, not until they find the man who kill Kelso."

"Then you will never live in the Grove," Fraser say.

"You are a contact man," Ram say, "which part you think I could get a room, boy?"

Fraser scratch his head. "I know of a landlord up the road who vow that he ain't ever taking anybody who come from the West Indies. But he don't mind taking Indians. He wouldn't know the difference when he see you is a Indian... them English people so foolish they believe every Indian come from India."

"You think I stand a chance?" Ram ask.

"Sure, you stand a chance. All you have to do is put on a turban."

"I never wear a turban in my life; I am a born Trinidadian, a real Creole. All the same, you best hads give me the address, I will pass around there later."

So Fraser give him the address, and Ram went on reading a few more boards, but he got discourage after a while and went to see the landlord.

The first thing the landlord ask him was: "What part of the world do you come from?"

"I am an Untouchable from the heart of India," Ram say. "I am looking for a single room. I dwelt on the banks of the Ganges. Not too expensive."

"But you are not in your national garments," the landlord say.

"When you are in Rome," Ram say, making it sound like an original statement, "do as the Romans do."

While the landlord sizing up Ram, an Indian tenant come up the steps to go inside. This fellar was Chandrilaboodoo (after this, we calling this man Chan) and he had a big beard with a hair-net over it, and he was wearing a turban. When he see Ram, he clasp his hands with the palms touching across his chest by way of greeting.

The old Ram catch on quick and do the same thing.

"*Acha, Hindustani,*" Chan say.

"*Acha, pilau, papadom, chickenvindaloo,*" Ram say desperately, hoping for the best.

Chan nod his head, say good morning to the landlord and went inside.

"That was a narrow shave," Ram thought, "I have to watch out for that man."

"That was Mr. Chan," the landlord say, "he is the only other Indian tenant I have at the moment. I have a single room for two pounds. Are you a student?"

"Who is not a student?" Ram say, getting into the mood of the thing. "Man is forever studying ways and means until he passes into the hands of Allah."

Well, to cut a long story short, Ram get a room on the first floor, right next door to Chan, and he move in that same evening.

But as the days going by, Ram had to live like cat-and-mouse with Chan. Every time he see Chan, he have to hide in case this man start up this Hindustani talk again, or start to ask him questions about Mother India. In fact, it begin to get on Ram nerves, and he decide that he had to do something.

"This house too small for the two of we," Ram say to himself, "one will have to go."

So Ram went down in the basement to see the landlord.

"I have the powers of the Occult," Ram say, "and I have come to warn you of this man Chan. He is not a good tenant. He keeps the bathroom dirty, he does not tidy up his room at all, and he is always chanting and saying his prayers loudly and disturbing the other tenants."

"I have had no complaints," the landlord say.

"But I am living next door to him," Ram say, "and if I concentrate my powers I can see through the wall. That man is a menace, and the best thing you can do is to give him notice. You have a good house here and it would be a pity to let one man spoil it for the other tenants."

"I will have a word with him about it," the landlord say.

Well, the next evening Ram was in his room when he hear a knock at the door. He run in the corner quick and stand upon his head, and say, "Come in."

The landlord come in.

"I am just practising my yoghourt," Ram say.

"I have had a word with Mr. Chan," the landlord say, "and I have reason to suspect that you have deceived me. You are not from India, you are from the West Indies."

Ram turn right-side up. "I am a citizen of the world," he say.

34

"You are flying false colours," the landlord say. "You do not burn incense like Mr. Chan, you do not dress like Mr. Chan, and you do not talk like Mr. Chan."

"Give me a break, old man," Ram say, falling back on the good old West Indian dialect.

"It is too late. You have already started to make trouble. You must go."

Well, the very next week find Ram out scouting again, giving the boards a perusal, and who he should chance to meet but Fraser.

He start to tell Fraser how life hard, how he had to keep dodging from this Chan fellar all the time, and it was pure torture.

"Listen," Fraser say, "you don't mean a big fellar with a beard, and he always wearing a turban?"

"That sound like him," Ram say. "You know him?"

"Know him!" Fraser say. "Man, that is a fellar from Jamaica who I send to that house to get a room!"

DORIS LESSING (1919–)
WAS BORN IN
KERMANSHAH, PERSIA,
AND LIVED IN
SOUTHERN RHODESIA
FROM 1924 TO 1949. IN
HER WORK, SHE OFTEN
DEVELOPS THE THEME
OF EXTRA-SENSORY
POWERS POSSESSED BY
MAD PEOPLE. LESSING'S
BOOKS INCLUDE
LANDLOCKED,
AFRICAN STORIES, AND
BRIEFING FOR A
DESCENT INTO HELL.

A ROOM

Doris Lessing

When I first came into this flat of four small boxlike rooms, the bedroom was painted pale pink, except for the fireplace wall, which had a fanciful pink-and-blue paper. The woodwork was a dark purple, almost black. This paint is sold by a big decorating shop in the West End and is called Bilberry.

Two girls had the flat before me. Very little money, obviously, because the carpeting was going into holes and the walls were decorated with travel posters. The woman upstairs told me they often had parties that lasted all night. "But I liked to hear them, I enjoy the sounds of life." She was reproachful. I don't have parties often enough for her. The girls left no forwarding address, following the tradition for this flat. Over the years it has often happened that the bell rings and people ask for "Angus Ferguson—I thought he lived here?" And the Maitlands? And Mrs. Dowland? And the young Caitsbys? All these people, and probably many others, have lived in this flat, and departed leaving nothing behind. I know nothing about them, nor does anyone else in the building, though some of them have lived here for years.

I found the pink too assertive, and after several mistakes settled on white walls, leaving the plum-colour, or Bilberry, woodwork. First I had grey curtains, then blue ones. My bed is under the window. There is a desk, which I had meant to write on, but it is always too cluttered with papers. So I write in the livingroom or on the kitchen table. But I spend a lot of time in the bedroom. Bed is the best place for reading, thinking, or doing nothing. It is my room; it is where I feel I live, though the shape is bad and there are things about it that can never be anything but ugly. For instance, the fireplace was of iron—a bulging, knobbed, ornamental black. The girls had left it as it was, using a small gas heater in the opening. Its heavy ugliness kept drawing my eyes towards it; and I painted a panel from the ceiling downwards in the dark plum colour, so that the fireplace and the small thick shelf over it would be absorbed. On either side of the panel, since I could not have the whole wall in plum, which at night looks black, were left two panels of the absurd wallpaper which has bright people like birds in pink-and-blue cages. The fireplace seemed less obtrusive, but my fire is a gas fire, a square solid shape of bronze, brought from an earlier flat where it did not look too bad. But it does not fit here at all. So the whole wall doesn't work, it fails to come off.

Another wall, the one beside my bed, is also deformed. Over the bed swells a grainy irregular lump two or more feet across. Someone — Angus Ferguson? The Maitlands? Mrs. Dowland? — attempted to replace falling plaster and made a hash of it. No professional plasterer could have got away with such a protuberance.

On the whole, this wall gives me pleasure: it reminds me of the irregular whitewashed walls of another house I lived in once. Probably I chose to paint this room white because I wanted to have the whitewashed lumpy walls of that early house repeated here in London?

The ceiling is a ceiling: flat, white, plain. It has a plaster border which is too heavy for the room and looks as if it might fall off easily. The whole building has a look of solid ugliness, but it was built cheap, and is not solid at all. For instance, walls, tapped, sound hollow; the plaster, when exposed, at once starts to trickle as if the walls were of loose sand held together by wallpaper. I can hear anything that goes on over my head, where the old woman who likes to hear a bit of life lives with her husband. She is Swedish, gives Swedish lessons. She dresses prettily, and looks a dear respectable old thing. Yet she is quite mad. Her door has four heavy, specially fitted locks inside, as well as bolts and bars. If I knock she opens the door on a chain four inches long and peers through to make sure that I (or they) will not attack her. Inside is a vision of neatness and order. She spends all day cleaning and arranging. When she can't find anything more to do in her flat she posts notices on the stairs saying: "Any person who drops rubbish on these stairs will be reported to the Authorities!" Then she visits every flat in turn (there are eight identical flats, one above the other) and says confidingly: "Of course the notice isn't meant for you."

Her husband works for an export firm and is away a good deal. When she expects him back, she dresses as carefully as a bride and goes off to meet him, blushing. On the nights he comes back from his trips the bed creaks over my head, and I hear them giggling.

They are an orderly couple, bed at eleven every night, up every morning at nine. As for myself, my life has no outward order and I like having them up there. Sometimes, when I've worked late, I hear them getting up and I think through my sleep or half-sleep: Good, the day's started, has it? And I drift back to semiconsciousness blended with their footsteps and the rattling of cups.

Sometimes, when I sleep in the afternoons, which I do because afternoon sleep is more interesting than night sleep, she takes a nap too. I think of her and of myself lying horizontally above each other, as if we were on two shelves.

When I lie down after lunch there is nothing unplanned about it. First I must feel the inner disturbance or alertness that is due to over-stimulation, or being a little sick or very tired. Then I darken the room, shut all the doors so the telephone won't wake me (though its distant ringing can be a welcome dream-progenitor) and I get into bed carefully, preserving the mood. It is these sleeps which help me with my work, telling me what to write or where I've gone wrong. And they save me from the fever of restlessness that comes from seeing too many people. I always drift off to sleep in the afternoons with the interest due to a long journey into the unknown, and the sleep is thin and extraordinary and takes me into regions hard to describe in a waking state.

But one afternoon there was no strange journey, nor was there useful information about my work. The sleep was so different from usual that for some time I thought I was awake.

I had been lying in the semidark, the curtains, of varying shades of dark blue, making a purply-moving shade. Outside it was a busy afternoon. I could hear sounds from the market underneath, and there was angry shouting, a quarrel of some kind, a man's voice and a woman's. I was looking at the fireplace and thinking how ugly it was, wondering what sort of person had deliberately chosen such a hideous shape of black iron. Though of course I had painted it over. Yes, whether I could afford it or not, I must get rid of the square bronze gas fire and find a prettier one. I saw the bronze shape had gone; there was a small black iron grate and a small fire in it, smoking. The smoke was coming into the room, and my eyes were sore.

The room was different; I felt chilled and estranged from myself as I looked. The walls had a paper whose general effect was a dingy brown, but looking closely at it I saw a small pattern of brownish-yellow leaves and brown stems. There were stains on it. The ceiling was yellowish and shiny from the smoke. There were some shreds of pinky-brown curtains at the windows with a tear in one so that the bottom edge hung down.

I was no longer lying on the bed, but sitting by the fire across the room, looking at the bed and at the window. Outside a shrill quarrel went on, the voices rising up from the street. I felt cold, I was shivering, and my eyes watered. In the little grate sat three small lumps of shiny coal, smoking dismally. Under me was a cushion or a folded coat, something like that. The room seemed much larger. Yes, it was a largish room. A chest of brown-varnished wood stain stood by the bed, which was low, a good foot lower than mine. There was a red army blanket stretched across the bed's foot. The recesses on either side of the fireplace had shallow wooden shelves down them, holding folded clothes, old magazines, crockery, a brown teapot. These things conveyed an atmosphere of thin poverty.

I was alone in the room, though someone was next door. I could hear sounds that made me unhappy, apprehensive. From upstairs a laugh, hostile to me. Was the old Swedish lady laughing? With whom? Had her husband come back suddenly?

I was desolate with loneliness that felt it would never be assuaged, no one would ever come to comfort me. I sat and looked at the bed which had the cheap red blanket on it that suggested illness, and sniffed because the smoke was tearing at the back of my throat. I was a child, I knew that. And that there was a war, something to do with war, war had something to do with this dream or memory — *whose*? I came back to my own room, lying on my bed, with silence upstairs and next door. I was alone in the flat, watching my soft dark blue curtains softly moving. I was filled with misery.

I left my pretty bedroom and made myself tea; then returned to draw the curtains and let the light in. I switched on the gas heater, which came up hot and red, driving the memory of cold away; and I looked behind its bronze efficiency into a grate that had not had coals in it, I knew, for years.

I have tried to dream myself back into that other room which is under this room, or beside it, or in it, or existing in someone's memory. Which war was it? Whose was the chilly poverty? And I would like to know more about the frightened little child. He (or she) must have been very small for the room to look so big. So far I have failed. Perhaps it was the quarrel outside in the street that . . . that *what*? And why?

L. P. HARTLEY (1895–
1972) WAS BORN IN
WHITTLESEY,
CAMBRIDGESHIRE,
ENGLAND. HIS FICTION
TENDS MORE TOWARD
ROMANCE, SATIRE, AND
PARABLE THAN TOWARD
REALISM. HARTLEY'S
SHORT STORIES ARE
BROUGHT TOGETHER IN
*THE COLLECTED
SHORT STORIES OF L. P.
HARTLEY,* AND HIS
NOVEL *THE
GO-BETWEEN* WAS
ADAPTED INTO A MOVIE
WITH A SCRIPT BY
HAROLD PINTER.

A HIGH DIVE

L. P. Hartley

The circus-manager was worried. Attendances had been falling off and such people as did come—children they were,
mostly—sat about listlessly, munching sweets or sucking
ices, sometimes talking to each other without so much as glancing
at the show. Only the young or little girls, who came to see the
ponies, betrayed any real interest. The clowns' jokes fell flat, for
they were the kind of jokes that used to raise a laugh before 1939,
after which critical date people's sense of humour seemed to have
changed, along with many other things about them. The circus-manager had
heard the word 'corny' flung about and didn't like it. What did they want?
Something that was, in his opinion, sillier and more pointless than the old jokes;
not a bull's-eye on the target of humour, but an outer or even a near-miss—
something that brought in the element of futility and that could be laughed at as
well as with: an unintentional joke against the joker. The clowns were quick
enough with their patter but it just didn't go down: there was too much sense in
their nonsense for an up-to-date audience, too much articulateness. They would
do better to talk gibberish, perhaps. Now they must change their style, and find
out what really did make people laugh, if people could be made to; but he, the
manager, was over fifty and never good himself at making jokes, even the
old-fashioned kind. What was this word that everyone was using—'sophisticated'? The audiences were too sophisticated, even the children were: they
seemed to have seen and heard all this before, even when they were too young to
have seen and heard it.

'What shall we do?' he asked his wife. They were standing under the Big Top,
which had just been put up, and wondering how many of the empty seats would

still be empty when they gave their first performance. 'We shall have to do something, or it's a bad look-out.'

'I don't see what we can do about the comic side,' she said. 'It may come right by itself. Fashions change, all sorts of old things have returned to favour, like old-time dances. But there's something we could do.'

'What's that?'

'Put on an act that's dangerous, really dangerous. Audiences are never bored by that. I know you don't like it, and no more do I, but when we had the Wall of Death—'

Her husband's big chest-muscles twitched under his thin shirt.

'You know what happened then.'

'Yes, but it wasn't our fault, we were in the clear.'

He shook his head.

'Those things upset everyone. I know the public came after it happened— they came in shoals, they came to see the place where someone had been killed. But our people got the needle and didn't give a good performance for I don't know how long. If you're proposing another Wall of Death I wouldn't stand for it —besides, where will you find a man to do it?—especially with a lion on his bike, which is the great attraction.'

'But other turns are dangerous too, as well as dangerous-looking. It's *being* dangerous that is the draw.'

'Then what do you suggest?'

Before she had time to answer a man came up to them.

'I hope I don't butt in,' he said, 'but there's a man outside who wants to speak to you.'

'What about?'

'I think he's looking for a job.'

'Bring him in,' said the manager.

The man appeared, led by his escort, who then went away. He was a tall, sandy-haired fellow with tawny leonine eyes and a straggling moustache. It wasn't easy to tell his age—he might have been about thirty-five. He pulled off his old brown corduroy cap and waited.

'I hear you want to take a job with us,' the manager said, while his wife tried to size up the newcomer. 'We're pretty full up, you know. We don't take on strangers as a rule. Have you any references?'

'No, sir.'

'Then I'm afraid we can't help you. But just for form's sake, what can you do?'

As if measuring its height the man cast up his eyes to the point where one of the two poles of the Big Top was embedded in the canvas.

'I can dive sixty feet into a tank eight foot long by four foot wide by four foot deep.'

The manager stared at him.

'Can you now?' he said. 'If so, you're the very man we want. Are you prepared to let us see you do it?'

'Yes,' the man said.

'And would you do it with petrol burning on the water?'

'Yes.'

'But have we got a tank?' the manager's wife asked.

'There's the old Mermaid's tank. It's just the thing. Get somebody to fetch it.'

While the tank was being brought the stranger looked about him.

'Thinking better of it?' said the manager.

'No, sir,' the man replied. 'I was thinking I should want some bathing-trunks.'

44

'We can soon fix you up with those,' the manager said. 'I'll show you where to change.'

Leaving the stranger somewhere out of sight, he came back to his wife.

'Do you think we ought to let him do it?' she asked.

'Well, it's his funeral. You wanted us to have a dangerous act, and now we've got it.'

'Yes, I know, but—' The rest was drowned by the rattle of the trolley bringing in the tank—a hollow, double cube like a sarcophagus. Mermaids in low relief sported on its leaden flanks. Grunting and muttering to each other the men slid it into position, a few feet from the pole. Then a length of hosepipe was fastened to a faucet, and soon they heard the sound of water swishing and gurgling in the tank.

'He's a long time changing,' said the manager's wife.

'Perhaps he's looking for a place to hide his money,' laughed her husband, and added, 'I think we'll give the petrol a miss.'

At length the man emerged from behind a screen, and slowly walked towards them. How tall he was, lanky and muscular. The hair on his body stuck out as if it had been combed. Hands on hips he stood beside them, his skin pimpled by goose-flesh. A fit of yawning overtook him.

'How do I get up?' he asked.

The manager was surprised, and pointed to the ladder. 'Unless you'd rather climb up, or be hauled up! You'll find a platform just below the top, to give you a foot-hold.'

He had started to go up the chromium-plated ladder when the manager's wife called after him: 'Are you still sure you want to do it?'

'Quite sure, madam.'

He was too tall to stand upright on the platform, the awning brushed his head. Crouching and swaying forty feet above them he swung his arms as though to test the air's resistance. Then he pitched forward into space, unseen by the manager's wife who looked the other way until she heard a splash and saw a thin sheet of bright water shooting up.

The man was standing breast-high in the tank. He swung himself over the edge and crossed the ring towards them, his body dripping, his wet feet caked with sawdust, his tawny eyes a little bloodshot.

'Bravo!' said the manager, taking his shiny hand. 'It's a first-rate act, that, and will put money in our pockets. What do you want for it, fifteen quid a week?'

The man shook his head. The water trickled from his matted hair on to his shoulders, oozed from his borrowed bathing-suit and made runnels down his sinewy thighs. A fine figure of a man: the women would like him.

'Well, twenty then.'

Still the man shook his head.

'Let's make it twenty-five. That's the most we give anyone.'

Except for the slow shaking of his head the man might not have heard. The circus-manager and his wife exchanged a rapid glance.

'Look here,' he said. 'Taking into account the draw your act is likely to be, we're going to make you a special offer—thirty pounds a week. All right?'

Had the man understood? He put his finger in his mouth and went on shaking his head slowly, more to himself than at them, and seemingly unconscious of the bargain that was being held out to him. When he still didn't answer, the knot of tension broke, and the manager said, in his ordinary, brisk voice,

'Then I'm afraid we can't do business. But just as a matter of interest, tell us why you turned down our excellent offer.'

The man drew a long breath and breaking his long silence said, 'It's the first time I done it and I didn't like it.'

With that he turned on his heel and straddling his long legs walked off unsteadily in the direction of the dressing-room.

The circus-manager and his wife stared at each other.

'It was the first time he'd done it,' she muttered. 'The first time.' Not knowing what to say to him, whether to praise, blame, scold or sympathize, they waited for him to come back, but he didn't come.

'I'll go and see if he's all right,' the circus-manager said. But in two minutes he was back again. 'He's not there,' he said. 'He must have slipped out the other way, the crack-brained fellow!'

EDNA O'BRIEN (1932-   )
WAS BORN IN
TUAMGRANEY, COUNTY
CLARE, IRELAND. THE
THEME OF SOLITUDE
EMERGES
THROUGHOUT HER
WORK, FROM *THE
COUNTRY GIRLS* TO
THE LOVE OBJECT AND
A PAGAN PLACE.
O'BRIEN'S NOVELS ARE
HAUNTED BY THE
IRELAND OF THE PAST,
WHICH SHE OFTEN
USES AS A
REPRESENTATION OF
THE WORLD-AT-LARGE.

MARY

Edna O'Brien

Dear Sadie
    I am in the toilet as it's the only place I get a bit of peace. She is calling me down to do the dinner as I am a good cook and she is not. He raised ructions yesterday about cabbage water and I got red and you won't believe it but he smiled straight into my face. He never smiles at her. If I tell you a secret don't tell anyone. She sees another man. Didn't I walk straight into them the night I was to meet Tom Dooley and he never came. Next day she gave me a frock of hers, I suppose so's I'd keep my mouth shut. And now I am in a fix because she expects me to wear it when I go dancing and I want to wear a frock of my own. It is brushed wool, mine is, and I know it is brushed wool but I am not telling her.

    Tom Dooley came the next night. He got the nights mixed up, a good job I was there. We went for a walk in the park opposite this house — there's a park, I told you that, didn't I? It's nice in the summer because there's a pavilion where they sell icecream and stuff but dead boring in the winter. Anyhow we had a walking race through the woods and he beat me blind and I got so winded I had to sit down and he sat next to me and put his arm around me. Then he kissed me and all of a sudden he raised the subject of SEX and I nearly died. I got such a fright that I took one leap off the seat and tore across the field and he tore after me and put his arms around me and then I burst out crying, I don't know why. And I had to come in home and when I did he was here by himself. She's always out. Goes to pubs on her own or wandering around the road gathering bits of branches saying how sad and how beautiful they are. Did you ever hear such nonsense in all your life. She wouldn't darn a sock. Anyhow he was here listening to music. He always is. And he called me in to warm my feet and sat me down and we hardly said one word except that he asked me was I all right and I had to say something, so I said I got a smut in my eye. Didn't he get an eye-glass and was poking away at it with a little paint brush and didn't she come in real quiet in her crêpe-soled shoes.

'Oh, togetherness,' she said in her waspy voice and you wouldn't see me flying up the stairs to bed. Next morning — and you mustn't breathe this to a soul — she was up at cock-crow. Said she had heartburn and went out to do some weeding. It's winter and there's nothing in those flower beds only clay. Guess what, wasn't she waiting for the postman and no sooner had he come than she was all smiles and making coffee and asking me what kind of dancing did I like, and didn't the phone ring and when she tripped off to answer it I had a gawk at the letter she got. I could only scan it. Real slop. It was from a man. It said darling be brave. See you a.m. Now I haven't told you this but I love their child. He has eyelashes as long as daisies and lovely and black. Like silk. I admired them one day and he wanted to pull one out for me. I'd do anything for that kid.

Anyhow I discovered where she keeps the letters — under the hall carpet. She presses flowers there too. Of course if I wanted to, I could show them to hubby, find them, pretend I didn't know what they were. I'm not sure whether I will or not. I heard him telling her once that he'd take the kid and go to Australia. I'd love to go. The kid has a pet name — he's called Buck — and he loves bread and jam and I think he prefers me to her. I have to go now as she's calling me. Not a word to my mother about this. I'll let you know developments.
Your fond friend
Mary

PS I am thinking of changing my name. How do you like the sound of Myrtle?

50

PART TWO
LOVERS AND HATERS

◆

GEORGE ELLIOTT IS A
CANADIAN WHOSE FIRST
COLLECTION OF
STORIES IS ENTITLED
THE KISSING MAN.

THE KISSING MAN

George Elliott

A real Gibson girl Froody was, before she got married. Think of the main street then: a blazing July sun draining the colour out of the buildings from the Queen's Hotel down to Geddes's dry-goods store. Then Froody comes around the corner at the Queen's. Graceful, elegant she walks, and cool. Cool black flowing skirt, finely pleated starched blouse, her hair done up and back in a neat, big pompadour with pearly shell combs.

She always used to wear white in summer, white starched blouses usually, with puffed sleeves and neat cuffs. Her skirts were dark, full-pleated and graceful, perfectly pressed. It was a pleasure to watch her walk down the street and into Geddes's store.

The men who hung around Weaver's barber shop across the street used to breathe a little heavier on purpose when they watched her. And they talked about her ears. It was a good thing she never heard about that or she'd have combed her hair differently and stopped all the nudging.

But the neatness of her was something different from being a Gibson girl. Maybe her mother insisted on the severe dark skirts and white blouses. Maybe her mother didn't realize Froody, in a get-up like that, was just what it took on a hot day to put gumption in a fellow.

Geddes's dry-goods was where she worked before she finally married Dougie Framingham. She waited on customers. She was good at it. Always polite, she addressed everybody as Mister or Missis, even though some of the customers were blood relatives of hers. It was Mr. Geddes's idea.

"Froody, you call everybody Mister or Missis," he said, "and they won't want to go and shop at the store down the street."

Froody was a dreamy girl. Sometimes it was a bother to her to keep her mind on the work. Usually she stood quietly in the narrow space between the two long mahogany show-cases that ran the length of the store. When there were customers to wait on, she drifted from one to the other as easy as you please.

"Not many real people come into the store any more," she said once. "There are weeks and weeks when I'm completely alone. I never see the customers as the people I know around town. They are there, and they're not there, kind of; without faces if you know what I mean."

"I'm not very tall," she said, "but I get this feeling I'm high up and the customers move along in the aisles away down out of reach. And sometimes I'm so thankful for it because that's where I want them to stay."

Somehow she always knew when she should snap out of it and start to be polite the way Mr. Geddes wanted her.

"You see a person moving closer to you, or you sense it I guess when you are clerking in a store," she said, "then you reach for the face and then reach for the name. After that it's easy."

Froody never knew it, but she wasn't like that to her customers — without a face. Froody was what was young and what was full of hope. Froody was proper beauty and proper beauty was becoming rare in town these days. Rare for most everybody. The only time you saw proper beauty was when Alison and Gerry gave one of their big parties in the drawing-room of the Queen's. Froody went to them with Dougie Framingham, chaperoned by her mother and father of course.

Well, it was a Thursday in July, the slowest day of the week, the slowest month of the year. There were only about ten women in the store. It was getting on for five o'clock. The kissing man opened the front door carefully and stepped in.

Mrs. Muncey was standing alone with her back to one of the show-cases, staring at the swatches of fabric fanned out on the long table next the wall. Her feet hurt, you could tell, and strings of greying hair had come loose and straggled on her shoulders. Geddes's was her last stop after doing all the stores in the block. Muncey, of course, was taking it easy in the cool of Weaver's barber shop. Mrs. Muncey was so tired she didn't turn around to see who it was when the kissing man came in.

The kissing man looked at her back for a long time. Tears came to his eyes. Then he walked right up beside Mrs. Muncey.

"You poor woman." His voice was a whisper, all compassion. Then he bent close to her and kissed her full on the mouth. His fingers touched her elbow for a moment. He walked out of the store. Nobody saw.

Mrs. Muncey could feel the weight of her sagging and knew her grey hair was straggling. "No, it's not. It's not fair at all," she said. She held to the show-case for support a moment, worked her lips in and out, then left the store.

At the back, Froody wondered what had gotten into Mrs. Muncey, letting the door slam like that.

That was all there was to it on Thursday.

Saturday is always the big day at Geddes's. The following Saturday, Aunt Cress went into Geddes's with Miss Corvill, the librarian at the time. Aunt Cress said the store was something like the street dance the Lodge puts on every fall: people chattering easily, a bustling back and forth, people helloing each other a little more than usual. It was like this every Saturday. Froody and Mr. Geddes were busy making out bills, making change at the old wind-up cash register, talking a little faster.

Miss Corvill was a pleasant enough woman, shy, not many friends. Nobody knew much about her, except that she was a cracking good librarian. This day she got separated from Aunt Cress in all those bustling women, so she stood idly fingering the texture of the different cloths spread on the table.

She had to turn around. She would never be able to tell why. She just had to. The kissing man was there close to her. All in his face was pity. He took her hand firmly in his two. He pressed her palm to his cheek.

"Oh God," he whispered, "why does it have to come to this?" His voice trailed off. He dropped her hand.

Who lived once, and was a person to love, now is a wisp of loneliness. Why is it that order of living, loving and loneliness? Why do I see it wherever I go? I dream of taking you, Miss Corvill, and loving your body with my eyes, touching you, making you cry for shame until the shame is out of you, making you cry then for that, and giving it, giving it all. The way no man ever did. It's the beginning. The beginning of life and love. And it's the end. The end of loneliness that leaves you dust. Why do I see it wherever I go? Living, loving and loneliness.

He left the store.

"Let's go home, Cressie, I'm so worn out from shopping. The heat and all. Let's go home." She knew her pince-nez hid the tears.

Froody saw it happen and wanted to scream out. Miss Corvill didn't seem shocked, angry or surprised. Froody wanted to ask her what he had said, but she didn't dare.

After Miss Corvill and Aunt Cress left the store, Froody reached out for the faces in the crowded store because a change had come over everything. It was now a barren orderliness: everything in place, everyone concentrating on their purchases, no more voices of excitement or welcoming happiness as people met in the crowded aisles. The warmth had gone.

That Saturday night Froody stayed in her room after supper and cried. She wanted to know, to get it, to share. It was all so hopeless.

Dougie Framingham showed up that night, as usual, and Froody told her mother to tell him to go away, that she wasn't able to see him. Later she came downstairs and found her mother pressing her father's Lodge sash. Her eyes lighted up and she thought of telling her mother again to stop it, that the Lodge wasn't worth it, that there was nothing to those men getting together except a band of thin cotton across still chests. She said nothing, though, because she saw her mother knew what she wanted to say. Froody sat on the bottom step of the stairs and watched.

"Muncey, Weaver and Sobel, Muncey, Weaver and Sobel," she said to herself. "Muncey, Weaver and Sobel, say them over and over again and nothing happens." She frowned at her mother's back and at the sash on the ironing-board.

The name of Muncey reminded Froody of Mrs. Muncey the past Thursday, slamming the front door at the store. Then the memory of the kissing man with Miss Corvill was bursting in her and stayed with her while she went upstairs to bed and until she fell asleep.

Next day she watched for the kissing man at church and she watched for him as she and Dougie drove sedately out to the town line and back in his rubber-tired buggy. She never saw him.

Monday was another hot, humid day, so there weren't many people in the store. Poor Mr. Geddes was so uncomfortable. He was much too fat for his age and he sat uneasily in a wicker porch chair that squeaked under his bulk. He stationed himself close to the window so he could see who was out on the street.

Froody was waiting on Mrs. Lalling, the widow who was on town relief. Mrs. Lalling was made small and hushed by the rich store atmosphere: that comfortable clothy smell, the old shining mahogany. She didn't like Mr. Geddes to be sitting there while she bought the few yards of print she needed. The height of the ceiling was an aching reminder that she was poor and shouldn't be in such luxury. She was nervous when Froody left her to go to the back of the store for some cloth. She wanted to leave then and knew she should have left at that very moment but she couldn't make her legs move.

The kissing man came in. He went by Mr. Geddes, past the long table and stopped. He looked to the back of the store where Froody had gone. Then he made Mrs. Lalling turn around. He pressed her close to him. Mrs. Lalling cried softly and gently.

He crooned, "Don't cry, don't cry."

Stepping into a dead man's shoes for a while, the body in earth out beyond the Fair Grounds, and she sits weary home alone.

Mr. Geddes hoisted himself up out of the chair and came to Mrs. Lalling. The kissing man ran to the back of the store. He reached the store-room door as Froody came out. He stopped.

"Mrs. Lalling is crying, isn't she?" Froody asked.

"Yes she is, poor soul."

"Why didn't you come to me?"

He went past her, towards the back door. Froody felt cold order coming on and the feeling of people without faces. She knew she would never see him again after this.

"You've been one of the lucky ones," he called back to her. "You haven't needed me yet."

She knew more then than she wanted to know, ever.

ERNEST HEMINGWAY
(1899–1967) WAS BORN IN
OAK PARK, ILLINOIS. HIS
LIFE AND FICTION
OVERLAPPED: BOTH
CONTAINED WAR,
SPORTS, DRINKING,
BRAWLING, AND
LOVING. HEMINGWAY'S
MAJOR NOVELS
INCLUDE *THE SUN
ALSO RISES, A
FAREWELL TO ARMS,*
AND *FOR WHOM THE
BELL TOLLS.*

UP IN MICHIGAN

Ernest Hemingway

J im Gilmore came to Hortons Bay from Canada. He bought the blacksmith shop from old man Horton. Jim was short and dark with big moustaches and big hands. He was a good horseshoer and did not look much like a blacksmith even with his leather apron on. He lived upstairs above the blacksmith shop and took his meals at D. J. Smith's.

Liz Coates worked for Smith's. Mrs. Smith, who was a very large clean woman, said Liz Coates was the neatest girl she'd ever seen. Liz had good legs and always wore clean gingham aprons and Jim noticed that her hair was always neat behind. He liked her face because it was so jolly but he never thought about her.

Liz liked Jim very much. She liked it the way he walked over from the shop and often went to the kitchen door to watch for him to start down the road. She liked it about his moustache. She liked it about how white his teeth were when he smiled. She liked it very much that he didn't look like a blacksmith. She liked it how much D. J. Smith and Mrs. Smith liked Jim. One day she found that she liked it the way the hair was black on his arms and how white they were above the tanned line when he washed up in the washbasin outside the house. Liking that made her feel funny.

Hortons Bay, the town, was only five houses on the main road between Boyne City and Charlevoix. There was the general store and post-office with a high false front and maybe a wagon hitched out in front, Smith's house, Stroud's house, Dillworth's house, Horton's house, and Van Hoosen's house. The houses were in a big grove of elm trees and the road was very sandy. Up the road a ways

59

was the Methodist church and down the road the other direction was the township school. The blacksmith shop was painted red and faced the school.

A steep sandy road ran down the hill to the bay through the timber. From Smith's back door you could look out across the woods that ran down to the lake and across the bay. It was very beautiful in the spring and summer, the bay blue and bright and usually whitecaps on the lake out beyond the point from the breeze blowing from Charlevoix and Lake Michigan. From Smith's back door Liz could see ore barges way out in the lake going toward Boyne City. When she looked at them they didn't seem to be moving at all but if she went in and dried some more dishes and then came out again they would be out of sight beyond the point.

All the time now Liz was thinking about Jim Gilmore. He didn't seem to notice her much. He talked about the shop to D. J. Smith and about the Republican Party and James G. Blaine. In the evenings he read *The Toledo Blade* and the Grand Rapids paper by the lamp in the front room or went out spearing fish in the bay with a jacklight with D. J. Smith. In the fall he and Smith and Charley Wyman took a wagon and tent, grub, axes, their rifles and two dogs and went on a trip to the pine plains beyond Vanderbilt deer hunting. Liz and Mrs. Smith were cooking for four days for them before they started. Liz wanted to make something special for Jim to take but she didn't finally because she was afraid to ask Mrs. Smith for the eggs and flour and afraid if she bought them Mrs. Smith would catch her cooking. It would have been all right with Mrs. Smith but Liz was afraid.

All the time Jim was gone on the deer hunting trip Liz thought about him. It was awful while he was gone. She couldn't sleep well from thinking about him but she discovered it was fun to think about him too. If she let herself go it was better. The night before they were to come back she didn't sleep at all, that is she didn't think she slept because it was all mixed up in a dream about not sleeping and really not sleeping. When she saw the wagon coming down the road she felt weak and sick sort of inside. She couldn't wait till she saw Jim and it seemed as though everything would be all right when he came. The wagon stopped outside under the big elm and Mrs. Smith and Liz went out. All the men had beards and there were three deer in the back of the wagon, their thin legs sticking stiff over the edge of the wagon box. Mrs. Smith kissed D. J. and he hugged her. Jim said 'Hello, Liz,' and grinned. Liz hadn't known just what would happen when Jim got back but she was sure it would be something. Nothing had happened. The men were just home, that was all. Jim pulled the burlap sacks off the deer and Liz looked at them. One was a big buck. It was stiff and hard to lift out of the wagon.

'Did you shoot it, Jim?' Liz asked.

'Yeah. Ain't it a beauty?' Jim got it on to his back to carry to the smokehouse.

That night Charley Wyman stayed to supper at Smith's. It was too late to get back to Charlevoix. The men washed up and waited in the front room for supper.

'Ain't there something left in that crock, Jimmy?' D. J. Smith asked, and Jim went out to the wagon in the barn and fetched in the jug of whisky the men had taken hunting with them. It was a four-gallon jug and there was quite a little slopped back and forth in the bottom. Jim took a long pull on his way back to the house. It was hard to lift such a big jug up to drink out of it. Some of the whisky ran down on his shirt front. The two men smiled when Jim came in with the jug. D. J. Smith sent for glasses and Liz brought them. D. J. poured out three big shots.

'Well, here's looking at you, D. J.,' said Charley Wyman.

'That damn big buck, Jimmy,' said D. J.

'Here's all the ones we missed, D. J.,' said Jim, and downed his liquor.

'Tastes good to a man.'

'Nothing like it this time of year for what ails you.'

'How about another, boys?'

'Here's how, D. J.'

'Down the creek, boys.'

'Here's to next year.'

Jim began to feel great. He loved the taste and the feel of whisky. He was glad to be back to a comfortable bed and warm food and the shop. He had another drink. The men came in to supper feeling hilarious but acting very respectable. Liz sat at the table after she put on the food and ate with the family. It was a good dinner. The men ate seriously. After supper they went into the front room again and Liz cleaned off with Mrs. Smith. Then Mrs. Smith went upstairs and pretty soon Smith came out and went upstairs too. Jim and Charley were still in the front room. Liz was sitting in the kitchen next to the stove pretending to read a book and thinking about Jim. She didn't want to go to bed yet because she knew Jim would be coming out and she wanted to see him as he went out so she could take the way he looked up to bed with her.

She was thinking about him hard and then Jim came out. His eyes were shining and his hair was a little rumpled. Liz looked down at her book. Jim came over back of her chair and stood there and she could feel him breathing and then he put his arms around her. Her breasts felt plump and firm and the nipples were erect under his hands. Liz was terribly frightened, no one had ever touched her, but she thought, 'He's come to me finally. He's really come.'

She held herself stiff because she was so frightened and did not know anything else to do and then Jim held her tight against the chair and kissed her. It was such a sharp, aching, hurting feeling that she thought she couldn't stand it. She felt Jim right through the back of the chair and she couldn't stand it and then something clicked inside of her and the feeling was warmer and softer. Jim held her tight hard against the chair and she wanted it now and Jim whispered, 'Come on for a walk.'

Liz took her coat off the peg on the kitchen wall and they went out the door. Jim had his arm around her and every little way they stopped and pressed against each other and Jim kissed her. There was no moon and they walked ankle-deep in the sandy road through the trees down to the dock and the warehouse on the bay. The water was lapping in the piles and the point was dark across the bay. It was cold but Liz was hot all over from being with Jim. They sat down in the shelter of the warehouse and Jim pulled Liz close to him. She was frightened. One of Jim's hands went inside her dress and stroked over her breast and the other hand was in her lap. She was very frightened and didn't know how he was going to go about things but she snuggled close to him. Then the hand that felt so big in her lap went away and was on her leg and started to move up it.

'Don't, Jim,' Liz said. Jim slid the hand farther up.

'You mustn't, Jim. You mustn't.' Neither Jim nor Jim's big hand paid any attention to her.

The boards were hard. Jim had her dress up and was trying to do something to her. She was frightened but she wanted it. She had to have it but it frightened her.

'You mustn't do it, Jim. You mustn't.'

61

'I got to. I'm going to. You know we got to.'

'No we haven't, Jim. We ain't got to. Oh, it isn't right. Oh, it's so big and it hurts so. You can't. Oh, Jim. Jim. Oh.'

The hemlock planks of the docks were hard and splintery and cold and Jim was heavy on her and he had hurt her. Liz pushed him, she was so uncomfortable and cramped. Jim was asleep. He wouldn't move. She worked out from under him and sat up and straightened her skirt and coat and tried to do something with her hair. Jim was sleeping with his mouth a little open. Liz leaned over and kissed him on the cheek. He was still asleep. She lifted his head a little and shook it. He rolled his head over and swallowed. Liz started to cry. She walked over to the edge of the dock and looked down to the water. There was a mist coming up from the bay. She was cold and miserable and everything felt gone. She walked back to where Jim was lying and shook him once to make sure. She was crying.

'Jim,' she said. 'Jim. Please, Jim.'

Jim stirred and curled a little tighter. Liz took off her coat and leaned over and covered him with it. She tucked it around him neatly and carefully. Then she walked across the dock and up the steep sandy road to go to bed. A cold mist was coming up through the woods from the bay.

SUZANNE JACOB IS A
QUEBEC POET AND
SONG AND
SHORT-FICTION WRITER
WHO LIVES IN
MONTREAL. "6550" IS
THE FIRST OF HER
MANY SHORT PIECES TO
BE TRANSLATED INTO
ENGLISH.

6550

Suzanne Jacob

Translated by Donald Winkler

I found a parking place just in front. That simplifies things because things are not simple. I took a good look at 6550, I wanted to pick out his window, but with 20 floors you have to calculate, you have to count up from the bottom, he lives on the 16th. The problem is that you never know if the ground floor counts for the first floor or if the first floor is called the ground floor. And when you count with your eyes, you're never sure that you haven't skipped a floor. Of course you can always count backwards beginning at the top, but you never really know where the 20th floor starts because there's often the floor for the swimming pool or the floor for the laundry room, you can never be too sure.

In any case I finished my cigarette, I put on my gloves, I did up my coat and I got out of the car. I locked it, you never know, even if I've got a little car on its last legs and all banged up, you never know, you never know anything very much.

Of course I should have phoned before coming this far, right in front of his place. But it's not always so simple, a simple phone call. Because I don't necessarily want my friend always to know where I'm going—just because he's my friend I don't have to tell him everything I do. When he's at home, even if he's fast asleep in bed, you never know, he could get up to pee or something like that and he'd hear me talking to someone and he'd ask who was on the telephone. It's not that he's especially jealous or that he wants to control me or anything like that, not at all, we're not possessive like that either one of us, he'd just ask out of habit, he always does. And since it would be perfectly useless for him to know Mike's name because it wouldn't mean anything to him, and since inevitably and as usual out of habit he'd ask who it was, and inevitably I'd tell him that it's nobody, because it really is nobody for him, it would all get complicated because things are complicated, and myself I prefer things to be simple. Even if that complicates my life a little, I prefer a complicated life to things being complicated.

But I could have telephoned him from the phone booth in the drugstore at the corner of the street. Yes, but the janitor is always there having a chat and he's very nice, he always wants to help me with something, he'd do anything for me. And if he saw me calling from the corner drugstore he'd certainly ask me if my phone was out of order and if he could do anything for me, anything at all. All things considered it's more practical to go and phone a bit further on. So I get into my car, it's always like that, and once I'm settled and I'm all warm at last and my seat belt is done up and my coat is arranged underneath me so as not to get wrinkled, I don't feel like getting out again to go and telephone because then you have to start all over.

In any case, I had arrived. In any case, once on the sidewalk I checked in my purse to see if I'd brought my address book because it happens to me more often than not that I forget it and then I have to wrack my brains to remember his apartment number because his apartment has four digits. I had my address book. There's a Murray's Restaurant just below 6550. That's lucky, it's practical for all sorts of reasons. I went up to the restaurant window where there were drawings of the things to eat inside and I checked the letter N to see if Mike was there. I really ought to work out a system for my address book and stick to it because the way I have of marking down sometimes first names, sometimes last names, makes me waste a ridiculous amount of time. When I look for Julie's number, for example, it's incredible the time I can waste. Because Julie's name used to be Julie Chavarie-Mathieu. Then she got divorced. Then she remarried and now she's called Julie Chavarie-Bourdais. With all these changes, how am I supposed to know where to look in my book?

In any case, Mike is not under N in my book, he's under M. I stuck my index finger in at the right page so as not to have to start all over once I found myself in front of the huge board with all the names and everything, it's amazing how many people live at 6550.

I pulled open the door. I checked my address book. His apartment number is 1614. I almost rang and then I told myself, better not do that. I stepped back a little so as to decide. It's true, that's not a way to behave. Everyone has his private life. You can't just burst in on somebody at any old hour on any old night of the week even if you have a so-called intimate relationship with the person in question. You can destroy someone's life forever by surprising him like that. There are things in life that are very delicate, and life is complicated enough without my taking it upon myself to complicate the lives of others, the lives of others are still part of life, after all. So I went out again and passed an old couple tottering along the icy sidewalk, they shouldn't be out in such weather, old people like that, it's not civilized that they should have to go out on a night like this, it must be an emergency, emergencies can't wait.

In any case I went into Murray's because I told myself there had to be a pay phone either at the back of the restaurant or in the entrance. There were two telephones in the entrance. If they had been visible from the street or from the sidewalk I wouldn't have hesitated to phone Mike before going into 6550. It wasn't too late and sure enough one of the two telephones was free, an old man was using the other, no doubt about it, he wasn't there to hide something from his wife or anything like that, he was making a perfectly ordinary telephone call right out in the open, he was talking loud, not too loud, but just enough so no one would hear me rehearsing what I would say to Mike, and that suited me fine. So I dialled Mike's number, I'd been holding it in my hand long enough, and I hung up right away, before it could ring at the other end. My heart was pounding because I didn't know any more what I wanted to say to him and how to tell him I was there and whether to pretend I was further away and let twenty minutes go by between the phone call and my buzzing him from the lobby.

I ordered a coffee to calm myself down a bit, coffee makes you nervous in general but it calms you down in particular, that's something you see all the time. And I ordered a roll, so as to catch my breath and make a final decision. I said to myself he's doing one of two things, either he's watching TV or he's puttering about. Puttering about, that means everything that isn't watching TV, that means everything besides the TV, all the rest. And you don't know Mike, but there are only two things in life that he doesn't find boring, he's a very serious person, it's only when he's working at the Research Institute or when he's screwing that he isn't bored. And when he's screwing he takes the telephone off the hook, and when he's at the Institute, he's not at home. By the time I'd thought all that out and nibbled at my roll, I felt much more calm. I knew that there was no risk in phoning him and that if he replied that would mean in any case that he was bored. I got up and I went to dial again the number in my book.

He answered. It was him, it was certainly him, I recognized his metallic voice. He sounded surprised, and when he's surprised his voice goes up one metallic notch. I asked if I was disturbing him, I always ask that, whatever I may think. He replied that I wasn't disturbing him at all, that he was bored and watching television, and he asked me where I was and where I was calling from and everything. I replied that I was at home, that was a lie, I couldn't do anything else, if I'd told him I was in the lobby he would have thought I was forcing him to invite me up, and if there's anything I can't do it's to oblige someone to make me an invitation, I just can't. That's something in my personality that I haven't analyzed yet, but I'll certainly get around to it, one always does.

Mike asked me if I was going to come over. He didn't ask me *to* come over, he asked me if I was going to. In other words, he didn't want to involve himself in my decision as to whether I'd go over or not. Mike is like that, he doesn't like to influence people. He doesn't say that it would please him or that he'd like it or that he needs it. It's a matter of independence, it's a kind of principle that he's always held to and there's no question of his ever changing it since he's always been like that and he doesn't like to try out other principles in general because he finds that where principles are concerned you have to have a very good reason to change them, especially when what's at stake is the independence of someone who has an average lifespan of sixty years.

I was accustomed to this character trait in Mike. That doesn't mean that it didn't disturb me, that it didn't bother me at all, on the contrary. But I let it go. I let a lot of things go, it's a way I have of simplifying.

For the moment, I saw myself up there already. I saw Mike exploring me through my coat because we'd have to get excited quickly because there wouldn't be much time given that Mike needs several hours of sleep, sound sleep, because he needs his rest for his work at the Research Institute, since it's with rest that one does one's research, that's what he says.

"Are you coming or not?"

It's clear, that kind of question. In my opinion, it's not very inviting. I've talked about it with others. With Pierre, for example. Pierre was of the opinion that it was just as inviting as anything else you might say.

Beside me, a big grey overcoat began to dial a number. I don't know what that did to me, seeing this grey unmoving overcoat dialling a number, I told Mike I was calling just like that, just to hear his voice, because it was cold outside and I felt lonely, but in fact I had absolutely no intention of going out, I told him that. He said we'd get together another time. We wished each other good night in voices that implied how well we remembered how it was when we went to bed together, and how it would be good when we could do it again, when the time was right. That's the sort of benediction conferred on me by the relationships I have with certain professional men.

I ran to my car, the wind was grabbing at me from every direction. I shut the door, I even locked it so the wind would stay locked outside and myself inside. I started the motor and the heater. When it was warm enough, I unbuttoned my coat. I didn't want to go home. I saw the traffic lights and I counted them. I'd wait until I felt like going back. I was sheltered from the wind. My gas tank was almost full. I had all the time in the world, I really did, all the time in the world.

ROBERT FONES LIVES IN
LONDON, ONTARIO, AND
IS THE AUTHOR OF *THE
FOREST CITY* (1974).
THIS STORY FIRST
APPEARED IN THE
MAGAZINE *WRITING*.

THE TURTLE

Robert Fones

At dusk the red light at the end of the cement pier began blinking on and off with a rhythm slower than the water lapping the sandy shore. Bugs swarmed for their final feeding before the all-night insanity of the mercury vapour lamps and bare light bulbs that illuminated The Bend.

Bobo sat on the edge of the sand dune just where it dropped down to the flat beach. Paths divided on either side of him going back to the waterfront cottages. Clumps of razor-edged grass grew out of small hummocks of sand held firm by intricate white roots exposed on the windward side. He scanned the horizon in all directions, finding nothing to stop his eyes but a few swimmers a long way down the beach. He heard her coming up behind him.

"Well, I'm ready to go."

Bobo turned around and looked at her. Something pushed him back against the sand and held his shoulders. The bully was sitting on his stomach, holding his arms down with his knees and slapping his face lightly.

"Okay," Bobo said, "I'm coming," and he stood up, brushed the sand off his shorts and followed her along the path. She had put on her black dress and nylons. Her hair was combed out straight and hung down almost to her waist. She was wearing make-up. She always dressed the same way when they went over to the main drag. It threw Bobo's mind into a black whirlpool. It reminded him of her wild past. She had been a member of a motorcycle gang. She had taken speed and could drink herself into oblivion given the opportunity. It was a part of her that Bobo couldn't cope with.

They walked across the cool lawn past the cottage that her parents owned. The man who rented the cottage next door was raking his poorly sodded yard.

"Going into town?" he asked.

"Yes," she replied petulantly. Bobo didn't say anything.

They walked down the road beside The Cut, across the bridge and turned down the main street. She waved to old friends, summer acquaintances. She laughed carelessly and tossed her hair over her shoulders with a characteristic shake of her head. Sometimes she smoked a cigarette. He smiled at her friends but didn't say anything because he didn't really know them or like them. He stared down the street toward the lake, feigning distraction whenever she stopped to talk with someone.

The Main Drag was a strip of asphalt about a quarter-mile long that paralleled The Cut, running back perpendicularly from the lake. Both sides were lined with hot-dog stands, roller rinks, miniature golf courses, penny arcades, a few midway rides and at the end nearest the lake the dance hall. Here the road curved left and made a long loop over toward The Cut and then joined back up with the main street.

An endless stream of cars cruised up and down the strip, taunted by teenage mermaids poised on parked cars. The sidewalks were crowded with tanned summer people, some residents, mostly vacationers. Occasionally there would be a nest of motorcycles with greasers standing around polishing chrome and combing their slick black hair. The police walked in pairs and one summer there was a riot. For Bobo it was a walk through hell. He was terrified of children, of greasers, of the underworld in general. The epitome of the underworld was the Dance Hall.

She knew some of the bands that played there. She knew some of the motorcycle gangs. She smoked cigarettes when she really wanted to show Bobo how wild she could be. It ate away at Bobo's brain. She talked about going to a dance. Maybe she would go sometime by herself, since he wouldn't take her. Bobo was terrified of the prospect. She would know people there. Boys would ask her to dance. She would get drunk and lose all sense of time and decency. She never remembered what happened to her when she was smashed.

Bobo didn't look at the faces of the crowd. He walked through the shuffling forms in a daze. At the end of the street the dance hall blared rock music and beckoned teenagers into its mysterious depths. Beyond the dance hall was a wide stretch of sandy beach. They walked down the cement steps over to a huge metal slide. Bobo was usually too keyed up to say anything. It was a mild purgatory to the hell he still had to face on the way back.

After they passed the roller rink and were almost back at the intersection of the main street and the highway, she stopped once again and began laughing and talking with a girlfriend. Bobo hung his head and followed the cracks in the flagstones. He heard a rustling noise and glanced over at the hedge which bordered the patio. He saw a turtle working its way out of the dense tangle of branches. He picked it up with both hands. Its legs struggled against his fingers. It had a hole drilled through the back edge of its shell and a short piece of string dangled from the knot that passed through the hole.

"A turtle!" she said, lifting her hands up to her cheeks. "Oh, let's take him home." Suddenly she was a little girl. The noise of the traffic faded. She wanted to hold it. Bobo handed the turtle over. She held it vertically, head up.

"Don't hold it like that," Bobo said.

"Why not?" she said. "They like to stand on their hind legs. Look, he likes me!" She laughed, almost hysterically. "Oh, he's sweet!"

She had a private understanding with animals. It was part of her other magical world that Bobo couldn't enter.

"Why should it like you?" he said.

"Because he told me," she said. "Look at the way he looks at me."

Bobo saw a terrified turtle struggling to get its feet on the ground.

"It just wants to get away," he said.

"Oh, let's take him home with us, can we?"

"Doesn't matter to me — only don't keep it in a shoe box tied with elastic bands like you did the last one."

"I didn't mean to kill it," she said seriously, then breaking into a grin: "I thought it wanted to hibernate."

They crossed the bridge and turned down the dark road that wound along the river. Yachts and cruisers were moored to the rickety wooden docks. The water was black, motionless. On the other side, behind the huge shady willows, the noise and lights of the main drag filtered through. Ahead of them, car headlights swept the sand and flashed momentarily in their eyes as they wheeled around the loop. They walked for a long time in silence.

"You don't like going into town, do you?" she said.

"I hate it."

"You don't have to come, you know."

"I know," he said.

"Did it upset you when I smoked that cigarette? Actually, I wouldn't mind one now. I wonder if Mark has any." Bobo drifted.

"Ow!"

The turtle dropped to the ground and pulled in its legs and head.

"What!"

"He bit me."

"How could he bite you, a little turtle?" Bobo kneeled down. "Poor thing."

"He did, right there." She showed him her finger.

"I don't see anything."

"Is he all right?" She took the turtle out of Bobo's hands and held it to her breast.

"Why don't you just let him go, he'd probably be a lot happier."

"He wants to be with me."

They continued along the road until the pavement stopped and a narrow gravel road curved uphill into trees and darkness.

"Let's take the path," she said.

They skirted the marina and walked along the cement retaining wall. The path appeared when the wall became too precarious to negotiate. They climbed up a long flight of white wooden stairs. There was a weak streetlamp at the top surrounded by moths and insects. Mark's cottage was ahead of them and to the right. He was unloading some things from his sportscar as they mounted the last step.

"Mark, look! We found a turtle!" She ran over to him, holding the turtle over her head — "except he hasn't come out since I dropped him."

She and Mark huddled over the turtle, talking quietly. She laughed. Bobo decided to avoid them. He crossed a little gravel road and went through the side gate into the backyard of her parents' cottage. He hesitated going into the house, decided instead to slip into the dug-out. The dug-out was a small cabin, about half the size of a one-car garage with a double bed at one end and a single bed against the other wall. Both cast iron with squeaky springs. Bobo threw himself down on the smaller bed. The mattress sagged and bounced a few times.

His skin was tight and itchy. His sunburn was becoming painful. He grabbed his notebook, switched on the bare light bulb and began writing:

Had a wonderful time tonight. She got dressed up and we drove over to The Bend and went to the dance. There was a really good rock band playing. The lead guitar was as good as Eric Clapton. Sue and Jack were there. We all had quite a few drinks and afterwards the four of us got into the car and drove north along the highway to a dirt road that led to a secluded part of the beach. We opened a mickey of scotch and passed it around until we were all laughing and totally smashed. Then we decided to go for a skinny dip so Jack and I dropped our shorts and sprinted into the lake. The girls hesitated but finally walked down to the shore with towels wrapped around them. We coaxed them in and they waded out to where Jack and I were. We played tag but we were so drunk we couldn't remember who was it and half the time I didn't have a clue who I was touching. Jack and Sue swam away from us and we crawled back up onto the beach and dried ourselves off. Then we made love right there in the middle of the fucking beach. It was beautiful and we just went on and on for hours. Finally we all drove back to The Bend and dropped Jack and Sue off at Sue's cottage before the two of us headed back to our place. What an evening! We both walked in and fell into bed and then she started. . . .

Bobo heard the screen door on the cottage slam. He knew she had gone in looking for him. He switched off the light. Moments later the door opened again, banged shut and he heard footsteps coming around the back of the cottage toward the dug-out. She opened the wooden slat door and leaned against the door jamb.

"What did you run off for?" she asked coldly.

"He's not really one of my friends," Bobo said. His head was reeling with jealousy.

"You could've been more polite."

Bobo didn't answer. He locked his hands behind his head and stared up at the rafters.

"Do you want to walk down to the pier or are you going to sleep?"

Bobo didn't move for a few minutes. He felt trapped. Then he slid his bare legs over the side of the bed. "No, I'll go," he said.

"Okay, I just want to change," she said and ran down the sidewalk in a flurry of crazy shadows and waving hair.

STEVEN SCHRADER, AN
AMERICAN, HAS
WRITTEN A BOOK
CALLED *ON SUNDAYS
WE VISIT THE IN-LAWS*.

WHOLE

Steven Schrader

The first morning I slipped off the ladder of my loft bed and landed on my ass. I cried. I cursed my ex-wife. Then I laughed. I flexed my ankles and stood up. My ass didn't fall off. I was whole.

I joined the block association to meet girls. They were all afraid of getting raped and mugged. A police captain came to the meeting and handed out whistles so the victim could blow it and summon neighbors. The girls collected money for brighter lights.

My wife missed me and we started sleeping together. It was just like a new girl friend. I left early before my son got up, so as not to confuse him.

It was a mild winter with many sunny, springlike days. Time didn't seem to pass. I was separated but I was still sleeping with my wife so I stopped. I needed change. I started sleeping with a girl in Riverdale. She was heavy and couldn't assume some of the athletic positions I was used to. On the other hand, I didn't have the warmth of Bernie, her previous boyfriend. We had awkward breakfasts on Sunday mornings. I wanted to rush away to visit my son, but I chewed toast and grinned. She smoked.

There was always snow on the ground in Riverdale. It never seemed to melt or get cleared away. People could ski. It was a resort area. I left and never returned. We spoke on the phone and became friends. You call me. I'll call you. Lose some weight. Develop some warmth.

I went to a party and fell in love. She was quiet and serene, the way my wife had been before she got angry. This girl had a boyfriend, though. Forget him, I told her. I'll show you a good time. Call me in a few weeks, she said. I'm tied up. I waited celibately. Almost. Just my wife a couple of times. She was there. It was convenient. My son saw me leave one morning and I said hello guiltily.

I cleaned my new place, bought some lamps and dishes and a rug. Never again with my wife.

I called the girl I loved but she was still tied up. You're not in love with him, I told her. You're too quiet. I could turn you on, perk you up. Theater, movies, and dance, songs and jokes. I'm terrific. She told me to call in a few months.

I bought colored sneakers and went to parties and danced for hours. I tried to connect. But the beautiful girls were all taken. And I hated the imperfect ones. One breast smaller than the other. Or else braces. I wanted a beautiful white smile. Now. I didn't want to wait two years for someone's bite to be corrected.

I went back to sleeping with my wife. In the morning my son came in and played on the bed and asked if I was moving back.

Spring came and I had to have extensive dental work. My teeth were okay but the gums had to go. I felt older. My body sagged. I was eating french fries too much, so I started cooking home. Lettuce and tomatoes. I learned macrobiotic cooking. I went to exercise class and took up yoga. My muscle tone changed. I was lean and wiry.

I fell in love with a young, beautiful girl back from England. She told me I had lovely muscles in my arms, a thick chest, flared nostrils, and distinguished features. We ran our bodies gently over our hands. I don't sleep with a man right away, she told me. Fine, take your time. A couple of years, decades, even. I can wait.

She broke the next date. I'm in love with someone else, she said.

I slept with my wife again.

What are you doing here, my son asked.

I fell in love with a girl who taught history in college. I want a relationship, I told her. Not just fucking. Communication. I'll try, she said. But I'm busy. I went to protests with her. Marched in the rain. Read the News of the Week in Review with her till three in the morning and fell asleep with a hard-on.

I answered a personal ad in a magazine, a mineralogist who wanted to meet people outside her field. She had nice breasts and a horrible twitch which distorted one side of her face. I started twitching, too.

Are you making fun of me?

No, I'm sorry. I can't help it.

We climbed up to my bed and made love on top of the sheets, in time to our twitches. At the end her twitch had stopped. She thanked me profusely.

I began answering lots of ads. None of those sensitive, nubile, whimsical, esthetic, artistic, and warm ladies mentioned their twitches or problems in the ads. But I discovered them right away. I laid my hand on their foreheads and took away birth marks. I cured stammers and club feet.

By summer I was tired. My apartment was steamy. My wife called and begged me to come over. I refused. I had my last personal to respond to. I was with a girl who wanted to kill her baby and I helped her throw it in the river.

That night I dreamed my wife had bought a gun and shot me. I woke with a pain in my stomach, the sheets red, and realized I was dying.

GWENDOLYN MACEWEN
(1941–) WAS BORN IN
TORONTO. IN HER
WRITING SHE COMBINES
RICH DESCRIPTIONS OF
LANDSCAPES WITH
EXPLORATIONS OF
TIME, MYTH, AND LOVE.
HER WORKS INCLUDE
THE SHADOW-MAKER, A
PLAY TRANSLATION OF
THE TROJAN WOMEN,
AND A CHILDREN'S
BOOK, *CHOCOLATE
MOOSE*.

SNOW

Gwendolyn MacEwen

She, of course, was used to it. Twenty-five years of parkas, furlined snowboots, mittens, scarves and crunching, slushing, sliding through it on the way to work or school. It was a Thing that covered the country four or five months a year, not unlike that billowy white corpuscle or whatever it was that went mad and smothered the villain of the film *Incredible Journey*. But for *him*, fresh from the Mediterranean, it was a kind of heavenly confetti, ambrosia or manna, and he rushed out half-mad at the first snowfall and lost himself in the sweet salt cold. He even dreamed of snow and he had a weird talent for predicting the next snowfall. He'd sleep and see tiny people coming down from the sky in parachutes that were snowflakes, a rain of infinitesimally small doves, ejaculations of white blossoms — the sperm of the great sleeping sky tree.

All through September and October his blood rose in anticipation of the cold, while all around him people lost their summer energy and grew weary and irritable as they thought of the long white siege ahead.

In December he trudged around frozen and delirious with joy in his soft Italian leather shoes with the pointed European toes, while she, bundled up to the chin with countless nameless pieces of wool and fur, hardly able to turn her head to see him, wondered how he could stand having to take his pants to the cleaner's twice a week to get the slush and wintry crud cleaned off of the cuffs. He made snowballs with his *bare hands*, if you can imagine, and when the tips of his ears turned a ghastly white from the cold, it never occurred to him to buy a hat. Coming indoors after an hour or two of strolling through a blizzard he would be *laughing* and freezing as if the winter were a great white clown someone had created solely for his amusement. She meanwhile, huddled in front of the oven or even the toaster, would try to unnerve him with horrendous tales of winter in Winnipeg. 'If you think *this* is something,' she would gasp, 'you should see what it's like out *west!*' and go on to describe how as a child she used to walk to school in the morning through shoulder-high snowbanks and by the time she got to the schoolyard there would be icicles in her nose and all round her mouth and her lips were so frozen she couldn't speak, and all the kids would be trying to laugh with their wooden lips. But he laughed too when he heard the story, and told her he wished he'd been with her out there, because, he explained, what thrilled him wasn't feeling the cold but letting the cold feel *him*.

Actually, she was quite a good sport with him that first winter he was in Kanada. At midnight after a heavy snowfall, they'd go into a little park where the swings and slides stood like skeletons in the blackness, and he, trembling with excitement, would put his foot into a fresh snowscape and examine the footprint of man marring the virgin whiteness. 'A giant step for mankind,' she'd say, as if the park were a moonscape, and slowly slowly they would walk forward pretending they were astronauts, clumsy and weightless in the midnight park, pouncing with glee on a swing or a slide or a water-fountain and radioing back to Earth that they had found evidence of an intelligent civilization. She would pick up a boulder—which turned out once to be somebody's frozen bowling shoe—and he, zooming in with his invisible TV camera, would relay the image to the millions of viewers in Tokyo and New York and Paris and London and Montreal. Then they would take imaginary pictures of each other standing triumphantly in front of the swings, or gazing rapturously at a gleaming slide, which seemed to be giving off inter-galactic signals, like the rectangular slab in *Space Odyssey*.

For the first half hour or so she found it fun; they made cryptic triangles and squares in the snow and she even taught him how to make an 'angel' by lying on his back in the snow and swinging his arms up and down on both sides. But he was always wanting to prolong the excursions long after the cold had crept into her bones and she, wet through and shivering horribly, would have to wait for him to finish his angels—sometimes five, six, even seven of them all done in a neat circle around the water-fountain with their wings facing many points of the compass.

Gradually they became quite serious about what they should make of each fresh snowscape. They would stand on the brink of the park sometimes for five or ten whole minutes debating what they should inscribe there with their feet or hands, not wanting to waste the cleanness, the newness of the snow on trivial ventures. Moonscapes and angels started to pall on them, so one night they decided to do a series of gigantic initials, which seemed easy but was actually quite difficult because they had to make tremendous Nureyev-like leaps between the bottom of an 'O' and the top of an 'R.' So he fell down flat in the middle of his name and got up protesting that it all came of not knowing how to write English well.

Another night they made a magic circle with segments bearing Cabbalistic Hebrew letters, and they both leapt into the centre of the circle and stood there under the stars and made secret wishes that are not our business to know.

Another night they were tired and spent the time throwing snowballs at tree trunks, which left hazy white circles like the fist-marks of avenging angels.

Another night they did Fantastic Footprints and Imaginary Beast tracks, trying to make the park look as if it had been the battleground between three-footed humans and hideous monsters who walked sideways like crabs. It took two hours to finish and though she had serious doubts as to whether it had been worth the effort, he was swollen with pride. You'd think he'd just completed a painting or a novel.

He was forever thinking up new things to be done with the snow. He considered (seriously) painting it, even flavouring it with sacks full of lime or lemon powder, and would have gone ahead with his plan had she not discouraged him by informing him you couldn't buy lime or lemon powder by the sack. So they made snowmen and snowwomen and snowchildren and snowanimals and snowstars. (A snowstar is a big ball of snow with long icicles—if you can find them—protruding out of the sides.) They made snowstars until her hands hurt. They made snow-trenches—where they lay in wait for the invisible army of abominable snowmen to come—until she thought she'd go mad, screaming mad. They made white fairy castles, they made white futuristic city-scapes, and they made footprints, footprints, footprints.

So I suppose what developed was, after all, to be expected. Which is not to say that she herself expected it in the least. When the night of the blizzard came and he hadn't showed up at his usual time, she got worried, very worried. And so she put on her fur-lined boots and her parka and her scarf and her mittens and went trudging out in the direction of the park. The snowfall that night was like a rapid descent of stars; they came down obliquely, razor-sharp, and her face stung and reddened and burned. *Snowfire*, she thought. Another word.

And she *was* surprised, though not totally, to find Grigori lying there at the bottom of the slide that gave off signals like the metal slab in *Space Odyssey*, with his Mediterranean hair all aflurry from the wind and his absolutely naked stone dead body wedged somehow into the snowdrift, and his arms outstretched at his sides as if he'd been making his last *angel*.

But what really got her was the smile on his face. He never did feel the cold.

_____

STEPHEN KING GREW
UP IN MAINE. HIS
BEST-KNOWN WORKS
ARE *CARRIE, 'SALEM'S
LOT,* AND *THE SHINING,*
AND HIS SHORT STORIES
HAVE APPEARED IN
PENTHOUSE AND
COSMOPOLITAN. HE
SAYS HE KNOWS THAT
ONE OF HIS STORIES IS
SUCCESSFUL IF IT
SCARES HIM WHEN HE
READS IT.

THE MAN WHO LOVED FLOWERS

Stephen King

O
n an early evening in May of 1963, a young man with his hand in his pocket walked briskly up New York's Third Avenue. The air was soft and beautiful, the sky was darkening by slow degrees from blue to the calm and lovely violet of dusk. There are people who love the city, and this was one of the nights that made them love it. Everyone standing in the doorways of the delicatessens and dry-cleaning shops and restaurants seemed to be smiling. An old lady pushing two bags of groceries in an old baby pram grinned at the young man and hailed him: "Hey, beautiful!" The young man gave her a half-smile and raised his hand in a wave.

She passed on her way, thinking: He's in love.

He had that look about him. He was dressed in a light gray suit, the narrow tie pulled down a little, his top collar button undone. His hair was dark and cut short. His complexion was fair, his eyes a light blue. Not an extraordinary face, but on this soft spring evening, on this avenue, in May of 1963, he *was* beautiful, and the old woman found herself thinking with a moment's sweet nostalgia that in spring anyone can be beautiful...if they're hurrying to meet the one of their dreams for dinner and maybe dancing after. Spring is the only season when nostalgia never seems to turn bitter, and she went on her way glad that she had spoken to him and glad he had returned the compliment by raising his hand in half-salute.

The young man crossed Sixty-third Street, walking with a bounce in his step and that same half-smile on his lips. Partway up the block, an old man stood beside a chipped green handcart filled with flowers — the predominant color was yellow; a yellow fever of jonquils and late crocuses. The old man also had

---

carnations and a few hothouse tea roses mostly yellow and white. He was eating a pretzel and listening to a bulky transistor radio that was sitting kitty-corner on his handcart.

The radio poured out bad news that no one listened to: a hammer murderer was still on the loose; JFK had declared that the situation in a little Asian country called Vietnam ("Viet-num" the guy reading the news called it) would bear watching; an unidentified woman had been pulled from the East River; a grand jury had failed to indict a crime overlord in the current city administration's war on heroin; the Russians had exploded a nuclear device. None of it seemed real, none of it seemed to matter. The air was soft and sweet. Two men with beer bellies stood outside a bakery, pitching nickels and ribbing each other. Spring trembled on the edge of summer, and in the city, summer is the season of dreams.

The young man passed the flower stand and the sound of the bad news faded. He hesitated, looked over his shoulder, and thought it over. He reached into his coat pocket and touched the something in there again. For a moment his face seemed puzzled, lonely, almost haunted, and then, as his hand left the pocket, it regained its former expression of eager expectation.

He turned back to the flower stand, smiling. He would bring her some flowers, that would please her. He loved to see her eyes light up with surprise and joy when he brought her a surprise—little things, because he was far from rich. A box of candy. A bracelet. Once only a bag of Valencia oranges, because he knew they were Norma's favorite.

"My young friend," the flower vendor said, as the man in the gray suit came back, running his eyes over the stock in the handcart. The vendor was maybe sixty-eight, wearing a torn gray knitted sweater and a soft cap in spite of the warmth of the evening. His face was a map of wrinkles, his eyes were deep in pouches, and a cigarette jittered between his fingers. But he also remembered how it was to be young in the spring—young and so much in love that you practically zoomed everywhere. The vendor's face was normally sour, but now he smiled a little, just as the old woman pushing the groceries had, because this guy was such an obvious case. He brushed pretzel crumbs from the front of his baggy sweater and thought: If this kid were sick, they'd have him in intensive care right now.

"How much are your flowers?" the young man asked.

"I'll make you up a nice bouquet for a dollar. Those tea roses, they're hothouse. Cost a little more, seventy cents apiece. I sell you half a dozen for three dollars and fifty cents."

"Expensive," the young man said.

"Nothing good comes cheap, my young friend. Didn't your mother ever teach you that?"

The young man grinned. "She might have mentioned it at that."

"Sure. Sure she did. I give you half a dozen, two red, two yellow, two white. Can't do no better than that, can I? Put in some baby's breath—they love that—and fill it out with some fern. Nice. Or you can have the bouquet for a dollar."

"They?" the young man asked, still smiling.

"My young friend," the flower vendor said, flicking his cigarette butt into the gutter and returning the smile, "no one buys flowers for themselves in May. It's like a national law, you understand what I mean?"

The young man thought of Norma, her happy, surprised eyes and her gentle smile, and he ducked his head a little. "I guess I do at that," he said.

86

"Sure you do. What do you say?"

"Well, what do *you* think?"

"I'm gonna tell you what I think. Hey! Advice is still free, isn't it?"

The young man smiled and said, "I guess it's the only thing left that is."

"You're damn tooting it is," the flower vendor said. "Okay, my young friend. If the flowers are for your mother, you get her the bouquet. A few jonquils, a few crocuses, some lily of the valley. She don't spoil it by saying, 'Oh Junior I love them how much did they cost oh that's too much don't you know enough not to throw your money around?'"

The young man threw his head back and laughed.

The vendor said, "But if it's your girl, that's a different thing, my son, and you know it. You bring her the tea roses and she don't turn into an accountant, you take my meaning? Hey! She's gonna throw her arms around your neck—"

"I'll take the tea roses," the young man said, and this time it was the flower vendor's turn to laugh. The two men pitching nickels glanced over, smiling.

"Hey, kid!" one of them called. "You wanna buy a weddin' ring cheap? I'll sell you mine . . . I don't want it no more."

The young man grinned and blushed to the roots of his dark hair.

The flower vendor picked out six tea roses, snipped the stems a little, spritzed them with water, and wrapped them in a large conical spill.

"Tonight's weather looks just the way you'd want it," the radio said. "Fair and mild, temps in the mid to upper sixties, perfect for a little rooftop stargazing, if you're the romantic type. Enjoy, Greater New York, enjoy!"

The flower vendor Scotch-taped the seam of the paper spill and advised the young man to tell his lady that a little sugar added to the water she put them in would preserve them longer.

"I'll tell her," the young man said. He held out a five-dollar bill. "Thank you."

"Just doing the job, my young friend," the vendor said, giving him a dollar and two quarters. His smile grew a bit sad. "Give her a kiss for me."

On the radio, the Four Seasons began singing "Sherry." The young man pocketed his change and went on up the street, eyes wide and alert and eager, looking not so much around him at the life ebbing and flowing up and down Third Avenue as inward and ahead, anticipating. But certain things did impinge: a mother pulling a baby in a wagon, the baby's face comically smeared with ice cream; a little girl jumping rope and singsonging out her rhyme: "Betty and Henry up in a tree, K-I-S-S-I-N-G! First comes love, then comes marriage, here comes Henry with a baby carriage!" Two women stood outside a washateria, smoking and comparing pregnancies. A group of men were looking in a hardware store window at a gigantic color TV with a four-figure price tag—a baseball game was on, and all the players' faces looked green. The playing field was a vague strawberry color, and the New York Mets were leading the Phillies by a score of six to one in the top of the ninth.

He walked on, carrying the flowers, unaware that the two women outside the washateria had stopped talking for a moment and had watched him wistfully as he walked by with his paper of tea roses; their days of receiving flowers were long over. He was unaware of a young traffic cop who stopped the cars at the intersection of Third and Sixty-ninth with a blast on his whistle to let him cross; the cop was engaged himself and recognized the dreamy expression on the young man's face from his own shaving mirror, where he had often seen it lately. He was unaware of the two teen-aged girls who passed him going the other way and then clutched themselves and giggled.

At Seventy-third Street he stopped and turned right. This street was a little darker, lined with brownstones and walk-down restaurants with Italian names. Three blocks down, a stickball game was going on in the fading light. The young man did not go that far; half a block down he turned into a narrow lane.

Now the stars were out, gleaming softly, and the lane was dark and shadowy, lined with vague shapes of garbage cans. The young man was alone now—no, not quite. A wavering yowl rose in the purple gloom, and the young man frowned. It was some tomcat's love song, and there was nothing pretty about *that.*

He walked more slowly, and glanced at his watch. It was quarter of eight and Norma should be just—

Then he saw her, coming toward him from the courtyard, wearing dark blue slacks and a sailor blouse that made his heart ache. It was always a surprise seeing her for the first time, it was always a sweet shock—she looked so *young.*

Now his smile shone out—*radiated* out, and he walked faster.

"Norma!" he said.

She looked up and smiled...but as they drew together, the smile faded.

His own smile trembled a little, and he felt a moment's disquiet. Her face over the sailor blouse suddenly seemed blurred. It was getting dark now...could he have been mistaken? Surely not. It *was* Norma.

"I brought you flowers," he said in a happy relief, and handed the paper spill to her.

She looked at them for a moment, smiled—and handed them back.

"Thank you, but you're mistaken," she said. "My name is—"

"Norma," he whispered, and pulled the short-handled hammer out of his coat pocket where it had been all along. "They're for you, Norma...it was always for you...all for you."

She backed away, her face a round white blur, her mouth an opening black O of terror, and she wasn't Norma, Norma was dead, she had been dead for ten years, and it didn't matter because she was going to scream and he swung the hammer to stop the scream, to kill the scream, and as he swung the hammer the spill of flowers fell out of his hand, the spill spilled and broke open, spilling red, white, and yellow tea roses beside the dented trash cans where cats made alien love in the dark, screaming in love, screaming, screaming.

He swung the hammer and she didn't scream, but she might scream because she wasn't Norma, none of them were Norma, and he swung the hammer, swung the hammer, swung the hammer. She wasn't Norma and so he swung the hammer, as he had done five other times.

Some unknown time later he slipped the hammer back into his inner coat pocket and backed away from the dark shadow sprawled on the cobblestones, away from the litter of tea roses by the garbage cans. He turned and left the narrow lane. It was full dark now. The stickball players had gone in. If there were bloodstains on his suit, they wouldn't show, not in the dark, not in the soft late spring dark, and her name had not been Norma but he knew what his name was. It was...was...

Love.

His name was love, and he walked these dark streets because Norma was waiting for him. And he would find her. Someday soon.

He began to smile. A bounce came into his step as he walked on down Seventy-third Street. A middle-aged married couple sitting on the steps of their building watched him go by, head cocked, eyes far away, a half-smile on his lips.

When he had passed by the woman said, "How come *you* never look that way anymore?"

"Huh?"

"Nothing," she said, but she watched the young man in the gray suit disappear into the gloom of the encroaching night and thought that if there was anything more beautiful than springtime, it was young love.

PART THREE
PARENTS, PARTNERS, AND PALS

◆

SHIRLEY JACKSON
(1919–65) WAS BORN IN
SAN FRANCISCO,
CALIFORNIA. HER
STORIES ARE NOTED
FOR THEIR
ATMOSPHERE OF
GOTHIC HORROR AND
BROODING FANTASY.
HER BOOKS INCLUDE
THE LOTTERY, AND
SUCH MACABRE WORKS
AS *THE HAUNTING OF
HILL HOUSE* AND *THE
BIRD'S NEST.*

CHARLES

Shirley Jackson

^{handwritten annotation:} foreshadowing in beginning paragraph / lacks disapline

The day my son Laurie started kindergarten he renounced corduroy overalls with bibs and began wearing blue jeans with a belt. I watched him go off the first morning with the older girl next door, seeing clearly that an era of my life was ended, my sweet-voiced nursery school tot replaced by a long-trousered, swaggering character who forgot to stop at the corner and wave good-bye to me.

He came home the same way, the front door slamming open, his hat on the floor, and the voice suddenly become raucous shouting, "Isn't anybody *here?*"

At lunch he spoke insolently to his father, spilled his baby sister's milk, and remarked that his teacher said we were not to take the name of the Lord in vain.

"How *was* school today?" I asked, elaborately casual.

"All right," he said.

"Did you learn anything?" his father asked.

Laurie regarded his father coldly. "I didn't learn nothing," he said.

"Anything," I said. "Didn't learn anything."

"The teacher spanked a boy, though," Laurie said, addressing his bread and butter. "For being fresh," he added, with his mouth full.

"What did he do?" I asked. "Who was it?"

Laurie thought. "It was Charles," he said. "He was fresh. The teacher spanked him and made him stand in a corner. He was awfully fresh."

"What did he do?" I asked again, but Laurie slid off his chair, took a cookie, and left, while his father was still saying, "See here, young man."

The next day Laurie remarked at lunch, as soon as he sat down, "Well, Charles was bad again today." He grinned enormously and said, "Today Charles hit the teacher."

"Good heavens," I said, mindful of the Lord's name. "I suppose he got spanked again?"

"He sure did," Laurie said. "Look up," he said to his father.

"What?" his father said, looking up.

"Look down," Laurie said. "Look at my thumb. Gee, you're dumb." He began to laugh insanely.

"Why did Charles hit the teacher?" I asked quickly.

"Because she tried to make him color with red crayons," Laurie said. "Charles wanted to color with green crayons so he hit the teacher and she spanked him and said nobody play with Charles but everybody did."

The third day—it was Wednesday of the first week—Charles bounced a see-saw on the head of a little girl and made her bleed, and the teacher made him stay inside all during recess. Thursday Charles had to stand in a corner during story-time because he kept pounding his feet on the floor. Friday Charles was deprived of blackboard privileges because he threw chalk.

On Saturday I remarked to my husband, "Do you think kindergarten is too unsettling for Laurie? All this toughness and bad grammar, and this Charles boy sounds like such a bad influence."

"It'll be all right," my husband said reassuringly. "Bound to be people like Charles in the world. Might as well meet them now as later."

On Monday Laurie came home late, full of news. "Charles," he shouted as he came up the hill; I was waiting anxiously on the front steps. "Charles," Laurie yelled all the way up the hill, "Charles was bad again."

"Come right in," I said, as soon as he came close enough. "Lunch is waiting."

"You know what Charles did?" he demanded, following me through the door. "Charles yelled so in school they sent a boy in from first grade to tell the teacher she had to make Charles keep quiet, and so Charles had to stay after school. And so all the children stayed to watch him."

"What did he do?" I asked.

"He just sat there," Laurie said, climbing into his chair at the table. "Hi, Pop, y'old dust mop."

"Charles had to stay after school today," I told my husband. "Everyone stayed with him."

"What does this Charles look like?" my husband asked Laurie. "What's his other name?"

"He's bigger than me," Laurie said. "And he doesn't have any rubbers and he doesn't ever wear a jacket."

Monday night was the first Parent-Teachers meeting, and only the fact that the baby had a cold kept me from going; I wanted passionately to meet Charles' mother. On Tuesday Laurie remarked suddenly, "Our teacher had a friend come to see her in school today."

"Charles's mother?" my husband and I asked simultaneously.

"Naaah," Laurie said scornfully. "It was a man who came and made us do exercises, we had to touch our toes. Look." He climbed down from his chair and squatted down and touched his toes. "Like this," he said. He got solemnly back into his chair and said, picking up his fork, "Charles didn't even *do* exercises."

"That's fine," I said heartily. "Didn't Charles want to do the exercises?"

"Naaah," Laurie said. "Charles was so fresh to the teacher's friend he wasn't *let* do exercises."

94

"Fresh again," I said.

"He kicked the teacher's friend," Laurie said. "The teacher's friend told Charles to touch his toes like I just did and Charles kicked him."

"What are they going to do about Charles, do you suppose?" Laurie's father asked him.

Laurie shrugged elaborately. "Throw him out of school, I guess," he said.

Wednesday and Thursday were routine; Charles yelled during story hour and hit a boy in the stomach and made him cry. On Friday Charles stayed after school again and so did all the other children.

With the third week of kindergarten Charles was an institution in our family; the baby was being a Charles when he filled his wagon full of mud and pulled it through the kitchen; even my husband, when he caught his elbow in the telephone cord and pulled telephone, ashtray, and a bowl of flowers off the table, said, after the first minute, "Looks like Charles."

During the third and fourth weeks it looked like a reformation in Charles; Laurie reported grimly at lunch on Thursday of the third week, "Charles was so good today the teacher gave him an apple."

"What?" I said, and my husband added warily, "You mean Charles?"

"Charles," Laurie said. "He gave the crayons around and he picked up the books afterward and the teacher said he was her helper."

"What happened?" I asked incredulously.

"He was her helper, that's all," Laurie said, and shrugged.

"Can this be true, about Charles?" I asked my husband that night. "Can something like this happen?"

"Wait and see," my husband said cynically. "When you've got a Charles to deal with, this may mean he's only plotting."

He seemed to be wrong. For over a week Charles was the teacher's helper; each day he handed things out and he picked things up; no one had to stay after school.

"The PTA meeting's next week again," I told my husband one evening. "I'm going to find Charles's mother there."

"Ask her what happened to Charles," my husband said. "I'd like to know."

"I'd like to know myself," I said.

On Friday of that week things were back to normal. "You know what Charles did today?" Laurie demanded at the lunch table, in a voice slightly awed. "He told a little girl to say a word and she said it and the teacher washed her mouth out with soap and Charles laughed."

"What word?" his father asked unwisely, and Laurie said, "I'll have to whisper it to you, it's so bad." He got down off his chair and went around to his father. His father bent his head down and Laurie whispered joyfully. His father's eyes widened.

"Did Charles tell the little girl to say *that?*" he asked respectfully.

"She said it *twice*," Laurie said. "Charles told her to say it *twice*."

"What happened to Charles?" my husband asked.

"Nothing," Laurie said. "He was passing out the crayons."

Monday morning Charles abandoned the little girl and said the evil word himself three or four times, getting his mouth washed out with soap each time. He also threw chalk.

My husband came to the door with me that evening as I set out for the PTA meeting. "Invite her over for a cup of tea after the meeting," he said. "I want to get a look at her."

"If only she's there," I said prayerfully.

"She'll be there," my husband said. "I don't see how they could hold a PTA meeting without Charles's mother."

At the meeting I sat restlessly, scanning each comfortable matronly face, trying to determine which one hid the secret of Charles. None of them looked to me haggard enough. No one stood up in the meeting and apologized for the way her son had been acting. No one mentioned Charles.

After the meeting I identified and sought out Laurie's kindergarten teacher. She had a plate with a cup of tea and a piece of chocolate cake; I had a plate with a cup of tea and a piece of marshmallow cake. We maneuvered up to one another cautiously, and smiled.

"I've been so anxious to meet you," I said. "I'm Laurie's mother."

"We're all so interested in Laurie," she said.

"Well, he certainly likes kindergarten," I said. "He talks about it all the time."

"We had a little trouble adjusting, the first week or so," she said primly, "but now he's a fine little helper. With occasional lapses, of course,"

"Laurie usually adjusts very quickly," I said. "I suppose this time it's Charles's influence."

"Charles?"

"Yes," I said, laughing, "you must have your hands full in that kindergarten, with Charles."

"Charles?" she said. "We don't have any Charles in the kindergarten."

96

JOHN CHEEVER (1912–)
WAS BORN IN QUINCY,
MASSACHUSETTS. HE IS
A SHREWD OBSERVER
OF SUBURBAN LIFE IN
AMERICA AND THE
DECAY IN MORAL
VALUES. HIS
*COLLECTED STORIES
OF JOHN CHEEVER* HAS
BEEN A POPULAR AS
WELL AS A CRITICAL
SUCCESS.

THE
FOURTH
ALARM

John Cheever

I sit in the sun drinking gin. It is ten in the morning. Sunday,
Mrs. Uxbridge is off somewhere with the children. Mrs.
Uxbridge is the housekeeper. She does the cooking and takes
care of Peter and Louise.

It is autumn. The leaves have turned. The morning is windless,
but the leaves fall by the hundreds. In order to see anything — a
leaf or a blade of grass — you have, I think, to know the keenness of
love. Mrs. Uxbridge is sixty-three, my wife is away, and Mrs.
Smithsonian (who lives on the other side of town) is seldom in the mood these
days, so I seem to miss some part of the morning as if the hour had a threshold or
a series of thresholds that I cannot cross. Passing a football might do it but Peter
is too young and my only football-playing neighbor goes to church.

My wife Bertha is expected on Monday. She comes out from the city on
Monday and returns on Tuesday. Bertha is a good-looking young woman with a
splendid figure. Her eyes, I think, are a little close together and she is sometimes peevish. When the children were young she had a peevish way of disciplin-
ing them. "If you don't eat the nice breakfast mummy has cooked for you before I
count three," she would say, "I will send you back to bed. One. Two. *Three....*" I
heard it again at dinner. "If you don't eat the nice dinner mummy has cooked for
you before I count three I will send you to bed without any supper. One. Two.
Three...." I heard it again. "If you don't pick up your toys before mummy
counts three mummy will throw them all away. One. Two. Three...." So it went
on through the bath and bedtime and one two three was their lullaby. I sometimes thought she must have learned to count when she was an infant and that

99

when the end came she would call a countdown for the Angel of Death. If you'll excuse me I'll get another glass of gin.

When the children were old enough to go to school, Bertha got a job teaching Social Studies in the sixth grade. This kept her occupied and happy and she said she had always wanted to be a teacher. She had a reputation for strictness. She wore dark clothes, dressed her hair simply, and expected contrition and obedience from her pupils. To vary her life she joined an amateur theatrical group. She played the maid in *Angel Street* and the old crone in *Desmonds Acres*. The friends she made in the theater were all pleasant people and I enjoyed taking her to their parties. It is important to know that Bertha does not drink. She will take a Dubonnet politely but she does not enjoy drinking.

Through her theatrical friends, she learned that a nude show called *Ozamanides II* was being cast. She told me this and everything that followed. Her teaching contract gave her ten days' sick leave, and claiming to be sick one day she went into New York. *Ozamanides* was being cast at a producer's office in midtown, where she found a line of a hundred or more men and women waiting to be interviewed. She took an unpaid bill out of her pocketbook, and waving this as if it were a letter she bucked the line saying: "Excuse me please, excuse me, I have an appointment. . . ." No one protested and she got quickly to the head of the line where a secretary took her name, Social Security number, etc. She was told to go into a cubicle and undress. She was then shown into an office where there were four men. The interview, considering the circumstances, was very circumspect. She was told that she would be nude throughout the performance. She would be expected to simulate or perform copulation twice during the performance and participate in a love pile that involved the audience.

I remember the night when she told me all of this. It was in our living room. The children had been put to bed. She was very happy. There was no question about that. "There I was naked," she said, "but I wasn't in the least embarrassed. The only thing that worried me was that my feet might get dirty. It was an old-fashioned kind of place with framed theater programs on the wall and a big photograph of Ethel Barrymore. There I sat naked in front of these strangers and I felt for the first time in my life that I'd found myself. I found myself in nakedness. I felt like a new woman, a better woman. To be naked and unashamed in front of strangers was one of the most exciting experiences I've ever had. . . ."

I didn't know what to do. I still don't know, on this Sunday morning, what I should have done. I guess I should have hit her. I said she couldn't do it. She said I couldn't stop her. I mentioned the children and she said this experience would make her a better mother. "When I took off my clothes," she said, "I felt as if I had rid myself of everything mean and small." Then I said she'd never get the job because of her appendicitis scar. A few minutes later the phone rang. It was the producer offering her a part. "Oh, I'm so happy," she said. "Oh, how wonderful and rich and strange life can be when you stop playing out the roles that your parents and their friends wrote out for you. I feel like an explorer."

The fitness of what I did then or rather left undone still confuses me. She broke her teaching contract, joined Equity, and began rehearsals. As soon as *Ozamanides* opened she hired Mrs. Uxbridge and took a hotel apartment near the theater. I asked for a divorce. She said she saw no reason for a divorce. Adultery and cruelty have well-marked courses of action but what can a man do when his wife wants to appear naked on the stage? When I was younger I had known some burlesque girls and some of them were married and had children. However, they did what Bertha was going to do only on the midnight Saturday show, and as I remember their husbands were third-string comedians and the kids always looked hungry.

A day or so later I went to a divorce lawyer. He said a consent decree was my only hope. There are no precedents for simulated carnality in public as grounds for divorce in New York State and no lawyer will take a divorce case without a precedent. Most of my friends were tactful about Bertha's new life. I suppose most of them went to see her, but I put it off for a month or more. Tickets were expensive and hard to get. It was snowing the night I went to the theater, or what had been the theater. The proscenium arch had been demolished, the set was a collection of used tires, and the only familiar features were the seats and the aisles. Theater audiences have always confused me. I suppose this is because you find an incomprehensible variety of types thrust into what was an essentially domestic and terribly ornate interior. There were all kinds there that night. Rock music was playing when I came in. It was that deafening old-fashioned kind of Rock they used to play in places like Arthur. At eight thirty the houselights dimmed, and the cast—there were fourteen—came down the aisles. Sure enough, they were all naked except Ozamanides, who wore a crown.

I can't describe the performance. Ozamanides had two sons, and I think he murdered them, but I'm not sure. The sex was general. Men and women embraced one another and Ozamanides embraced several men. At one point a stranger, sitting in the seat on my right, put his hand on my knee. I didn't want to reproach him for a human condition, nor did I want to encourage him. I removed his hand and experienced a deep nostalgia for the innocent movie theaters of my youth. In the little town where I was raised there was one—The Alhambra. My favorite movie was called *The Fourth Alarm*. I saw it first one Tuesday after school and stayed on for the evening show. My parents worried when I didn't come home for supper and I was scolded. On Wednesday I played hooky and was able to see the show twice and get home in time for supper. I went to school on Thursday but I went to the theater as soon as school closed and sat partway through the evening show. My parents must have called the police, because a patrolman came into the theater and made me go home. I was forbidden to go to the theater on Friday, but I spent all Saturday there, and on Saturday the picture ended its run. The picture was about the substitution of automobiles for horse-drawn fire engines. Four fire companies were involved. Three of the teams had been replaced by engines and the miserable horses had been sold to brutes. One team remained, but its days were numbered. The men and the horses were sad. Then suddenly there was a great fire. One saw the first engine, the second, and the third race off to the conflagration. Back at the horse-drawn company, things were very gloomy. Then the fourth alarm rang— it was their summons—and they sprang into action, harnessed the team, and galloped across the city. They put out the fire, saved the city, and were given an amnesty by the mayor. Now on the stage Ozamanides was writing something obscene on my wife's buttocks.

Had nakedness—its thrill—annihilated her sense of nostalgia? Nostalgia—in spite of her close-set eyes—was one of her principal charms. It was her gift gracefully to carry the memory of some experience into another tense. Did she, mounted in public by a naked stranger, remember any of the places where we had made love—the rented houses close to the sea, where one heard in the sounds of a summer rain the prehistoric promises of love, peacefulness, and beauty? Should I stand up in the theater and shout for her to return, return, return in the name of love, humor, and serenity? It was nice driving home after parties in the snow, I thought. The snow flew into the headlights and made it

101

seem as if we were going a hundred miles an hour. It was nice driving home in the snow after parties. Then the cast lined up and urged us — commanded us in fact — to undress and join them.

This seemed to be my duty. How else could I approach understanding Bertha? I've always been very quick to get out of my clothes. I did. However, there was a problem. What should I do with my wallet, wristwatch, and car keys? I couldn't safely leave them in my clothes. So, naked, I started down the aisle with my valuables in my right hand. As I came up to the action a naked young man stopped me and shouted — sang — "Put down your lendings. Lendings are impure."

"But it's my wallet and my watch and the car keys," I said.

"Put down your lendings," he sang.

"But I have to drive home from the station," I said, "and I have sixty or seventy dollars in cash."

"Put down your lendings."

"I can't, I really can't. I have to eat and drink and get home."

"Put down your lendings."

Then one by one they all, including Bertha, picked up the incantation. The whole cast began to chant: "Put down your lendings, put down your lendings."

The sense of being unwanted has always been for me acutely painful. I suppose some clinician would have an explanation. The sensation is reverberative and seems to attach itself as the last link in a chain made up of all similar experience. The voices of the cast were loud and scornful, and there I was, buck naked, somewhere in the middle of the city and unwanted, remembering missed football tackles, lost fights, the contempt of strangers, the sound of laughter from behind shut doors. I held my valuables in my right hand, my literal identification. None of it was irreplaceable, but to cast it off would seem to threaten my essence, the shadow of myself that I could see on the floor, my name.

I went back to my seat and got dressed. This was difficult in such a cramped space. The cast was still shouting. Walking up the sloping aisle of the ruined theater was powerfully reminiscent. I had made the same gentle ascent after *King Lear* and *The Cherry Orchard*. I went outside.

It was still snowing. It looked like a blizzard. A cab was stuck in front of the theater and I remembered then that I had snow tires. This gave me a sense of security and accomplishment that would have disgusted Ozamanides and his naked court; but I seemed not to have exposed my inhibitions but to have hit on some marvelously practical and obdurate part of myself. The wind flung the snow into my face and so, singing and jingling the car keys, I walked to the train.

FREDERIC RAPHAEL
(1931 –   ) WAS BORN IN
CHICAGO, ILLINOIS, AND
EDUCATED IN ENGLAND
AT CAMBRIDGE. "FOR
ME," SAYS RAPHAEL,
"THE NOVELIST IS,
ABOVE ALL, THE
HISTORIAN OF
CONSCIENCE." HIS
BOOKS INCLUDE
*LINDMANN,
ORCHESTRA AND
BEGINNERS,* AND *LIKE
MEN BETRAYED.*

BRIDAL
SUITE

Frederic Raphael

S trange things honeymoons,' he said to her in the limousine on the way to the airport.

'Stranger still,' she said, 'when you've been together as long as we have.'

'I sure hope we did the right thing,' he said, when Central American Airways called the flight.

'Getting married?' she said. 'Not much we can do about it now. We already ate the cake.'

'Maybe we did,' he said, 'but do we have to fly to the dysentery belt to blow out the candles?'

'You seem different,' she said, with a smile to prove she wasn't.

'Maybe I am,' he said, 'I was never married before.'

'I was,' she said. 'And please don't be. Different. I like you the way you were.'

'That was yesterday,' he said, and seemed to resent the way she helped him fasten his safety belt.

He had known her three, going on four years. He had always thought her face unique for its wide blue eyes and its white, incisive teeth above that neat, narrow jaw. It was rather a shock to observe, at the wedding breakfast, that she had three sisters and, almost more disconcerting, two brothers (Alvin and MacMichael, for God's sakes), all of whom had the eyes and the teeth and the neat, narrow jaw.

They were going only two and a bit hours from Dallas, but the faces in the jet were mainly swarthy; the Spanish announcements were more clearly understood than the English. He just hoped that the hotel was going to be all right. It

---

was American-owned, but he still thought maybe the whole thing was a mistake. 'The honeymoon,' he meant, 'not the wedding.'

They drove at last into the modern section of the city, concretely rebuilt since the recent earthquake, along a fancy avenue named after the American president whose vice-president had had to dodge the stones of the mob on his way to the *casa del presidente* where the prevailing general had taken receipt of the funds for the construction of the highway. The general now lived in some luxury in Lucerne; the highway was not as long as the purse allotted to it.

There was nothing obviously wrong with the hotel. It had a coffee shop and a gourmet restaurant and a heated pool and two hire car desks and there were tours available to the unspoiled hinterland. The bridal suite was on the seventh floor and it was already embarrassingly effusive with flowers and good wishes from the folks they hoped they had left behind. The management had been thoughtful with fruit. She watched, dismayed at his dismay, as he winced at the florists' cellophane. She wished that they were back at the twelve bucks a night motel where the affair began, in a place called Alexandria, Louisiana. It had been a hundred and fifteen in the shade when they checked in and the shower wasn't working and who cared? Now she took a shower, but he didn't seem to want to come in and get anything. She came out and he was standing at the window looking down, without enthusiasm, on the crowded evening buses taking workers back to their shanties. The sides of the buses were badged with the portraits of the new generation of contending generals who hoped one day, if elected, to live in Lucerne.

The hotel promised American service, but it was staffed mainly by local Indians. There was trouble getting a drink; there was more trouble obtaining a sandwich. As darkness fell, the sky was luminous with flashes. They heard distant explosions. 'Sounds like they have a fiesta going on,' she said. 'I hate fiestas,' he said, and made it sound as though he also hated her. She wriggled silken toes and smoothed her stockings up her gleaming thighs. He stared out of the window. 'We're going to have folksongs next,' he said, 'you wait and see.' He sighed as a crackle of festive fire made him flinch. He opened the terrace window and stepped into the flashing night. She followed him, accepting an invitation which had not been offered. The sky was splenetic with low and temporary constellations. The evening air prickled in her nostrils like a summer cold. She stood by her husband and willed him to admire the gaudy dazzle of the city.

Suddenly a mass of people, shouting and waving things, came running out of a side street opposite the hotel and spilled into the avenue. They were followed by a squad of masked and shielded police who seemed rather comically slow on cue as they began, with no evident order or purpose, to fire into the crowd. People screamed and ran in various directions. From the high terrace they could look directly down to where two men were being thumped with rifle butts as they slid down the railings of the hotel compound, access to which was blocked by a limousine carrying a diplomatic quartet.

She looked down then with appalled condescension at the bloody scene below them. In the distance, as she glanced away, she could see the trickling raw redness of a volcano, like a picked scab against the far sky. Her throat was sour with the tear-gas which, even at the height of the seventh floor, rasped her lungs. 'You're right,' she said, 'we have to get out of here; it's horrible.' Fear and revulsion made uneasy stilts of the high heels she had decided to put on. She leaned her head on his shoulder, for help. His arms promptly bracketed her, his hands hard where she was soft. She wanted to go in, out of the vicious dark, but

106

he held her there on the terrace, while the violence from the street rose like a savage drug. She shook her head — no, not now — but he was smiling. 'It *is* our honeymoon,' he said.

MARGARET ATWOOD
(1939–) WAS BORN IN
OTTAWA, ONTARIO, AND
IS A POET, NOVELIST,
AND CRITIC. HER
CRITICAL SURVEY OF
CANADIAN LITERATURE,
SURVIVAL, HAS A WIDE
FOLLOWING, AS DO HER
MANY BOOKS OF
POETRY, THE MOST
RECENT OF WHICH IS
TRUE STORIES. HER
TWO LATEST NOVELS,
LADY ORACLE AND
LIFE BEFORE MAN,
EXPLORE THE THEMES
OF LOVE, MARRIAGE,
AND THE SEARCH FOR
IDENTITY.

GIVING BIRTH
(excerpt)

Margaret Atwood

J eannie tries to reach down to the baby, as she has many times before, sending waves of love, colour, music, down through her arteries to it, but she finds she can no longer do this. She can no longer feel the baby as a baby, its arms and legs poking, kicking, turning. It has collected itself together, it's a hard sphere, it does not have time right now to listen to her. She's grateful for this because she isn't sure anyway how good the message would be. She no longer has control of the numbers either, she can no longer see them, although she continues mechanically to count. She realizes she has practised for the wrong thing, A. squeezing her knee was nothing, she should have practised for this, whatever it is.

"Slow down," A. says. She's on her side now, he's holding her hand. "Slow it right down."

"I can't, I can't do it, I can't do this."

"Yes you can."

"Will I sound like that?"

"Like what?" A. says. Perhaps he can't hear it: it's the other woman, in the room next door or the room next door to that. She's screaming and crying, screaming and crying. While she cries she is saying, over and over, "It hurts. It hurts."

"No, you won't," he says. So there is someone, after all.

A doctor comes in, not her own doctor. They want her to turn over on her back.

"I can't," she says. "I don't like it that way." Sounds have receded, she has trouble hearing them. She turns over and the doctor gropes with her rubber-gloved hand. Something wet and hot flows over her thighs.

"It was just ready to break," the doctor says. "All I had to do was touch it. Four centimetres," she says to A.

"Only *four?*" Jeannie says. She feels cheated; they must be wrong. The doctor says her own doctor will be called in time. Jeannie is outraged at them. They have not understood, but it's too late to say this and she slips back into the dark place, which is not hell, which is more like being inside, trying to get out. *Out,* she says or thinks. Then she is floating, the numbers are gone, if anyone told her to get up, go out of the room, stand on her head, she would do it. From minute to minute she comes up again, grabs for air.

"You're hyperventilating," A. says. "Slow it down." He is rubbing her back now, hard, and she takes his hand and shoves it viciously farther down, to the right place, which is not the right place as soon as his hand is there. She remembers a story she read once, about the Nazis tying the legs of Jewish women together during labour. She never really understood before how that could kill you.

A nurse appears with a needle. "I don't want it," Jeannie says.

"Don't be hard on yourself," the nurse says. "You don't have to go through pain like that." *What pain?* Jeannie thinks. When there is no pain she feels nothing, when there is pain, she feels nothing because there is no *she*. This, finally, is the disappearance of language. *You don't remember afterwards*, she has been told by almost everyone.

Jeannie comes out of a contraction, gropes for control. "Will it hurt the baby?" she says.

"It's a mild analgesic," the doctor says. "We wouldn't allow anything that would hurt the baby." Jeannie doesn't believe this. Nevertheless she is jabbed, and the doctor is right, it is very mild, because it doesn't seem to do a thing for Jeannie, though A. later tells her she has slept briefly between contractions.

Suddenly she sits bolt upright. She is wide awake and lucid. "You have to ring that bell right now," she says. "This baby is being born."

A. clearly doesn't believe her. "I can feel it, I can feel the head," she says. A. pushes the button for the call bell. A nurse appears and checks, and now everything is happening too soon, nobody is ready. They set off down the hall, the nurse wheeling. Jeannie feels fine. She watches the corridors, the edges of everything shadowy because she doesn't have her glasses on. She hopes A. will remember to bring them. They pass another doctor.

"Need me?" she asks.

"Oh no," the nurse answers breezily. "Natural childbirth."

Jeannie realizes that this woman must have been the anaesthetist. "What?" she says, but it's too late now, they are in the room itself, all those glossy surfaces, tubular strange apparatus like a science fiction movie, and the nurse is telling her to get onto the delivery table. No one else is in the room.

"You must be crazy," Jeannie says.

"Don't push," the nurse says.

"What do you mean?" Jeannie says. This is absurd. Why should she wait, why should the baby wait for them because they're late?

"Breathe through your mouth," the nurse says. "Pant," and Jeannie finally remembers how. When the contraction is over she uses the nurse's arm as a lever and hauls herself across onto the table.

From somewhere her own doctor materializes, in her doctor suit already, looking even more like Mary Poppins than usual, and Jeannie says, "Bet you weren't expecting to see me so soon!" The baby is being born when Jeannie said it would, though just three days ago the doctor said it would be at least another week, and this makes Jeannie feel jubilant and smug. Not that she knew, she'd believed the doctor.

She's being covered with a green tablecloth, they are taking far too long, she feels like pushing the baby out now, before they are ready. A. is there by her head, swathed in robes, hats, masks. He has forgotten her glasses. "Push now," the doctor says. Jeannie grips with her hands, grits her teeth, face, her whole body together, a snarl, a fierce smile, the baby is enormous, a stone, a boulder, her bones unlock, and once, twice, the third time, she opens like a birdcage turning slowly inside out.

A pause; a wet kitten slithers between her legs. "Why don't you look?" says the doctor, but Jeannie still has her eyes closed. No glasses, she couldn't have seen a thing anyway. "Why don't you look?" the doctor says again.

Jeannie opens her eyes. She can see the baby, who has been wheeled up beside her and is fading already from the alarming birth purple. *A good baby,* she thinks, meaning it as the old woman did: *a good watch,* well-made, substantial. The baby isn't crying; she squints in the new light. Birth isn't something that has been given to her, nor has she taken it. It was just something that has happened so they could greet each other like this. The nurse is stringing beads for her name. When the baby is bundled and tucked beside Jeannie, she goes to sleep.

RICHARD BRAUTIGAN
(1933-) WAS BORN IN
TACOMA, WASHINGTON.
HE HAS FOUND A WAY TO
MAKE AMERICANS
BELIEVE ONCE MORE IN
THE ORIGINAL SPIRIT OF
THEIR COUNTRY. HIS
STORIES APPEAR IN
*REVENGE OF THE
LAWN,* AND HIS BETTER
KNOWN NOVELS
INCLUDE *A
CONFEDERATE
GENERAL FROM BIG
SUR* AND *TROUT
FISHING IN AMERICA.*

THE
WORLD WAR I
LOS ANGELES
AIRPLANE

Richard Brautigan

He was found lying dead near the television set on the front room floor of a small rented house in Los Angeles. My wife had gone to the store to get some ice cream. It was an early-in-the-night-just-a-few-blocks-away store. We were in an ice-cream mood. The telephone rang. It was her brother to say that her father had died that afternoon. He was seventy. I waited for her to come home with the ice cream. I tried to think of the best way to tell her that her father was dead with the least amount of pain but you cannot camouflage death with words. Always at the end of the words somebody is dead.

She was very happy when she came back from the store.

"What's wrong?" she said.

"Your brother just called from Los Angeles," I said.

"What happened?" she said.

"Your father died this afternoon."

That was in 1960 and now it's just a few weeks away from 1970. He has been dead for almost ten years and I've done a lot of thinking about what his death means to all of us.

1. He was born from German blood and raised on a farm in South Dakota. His grandfather was a terrible tyrant who completely destroyed his three grown sons by treating them exactly the way he treated them when they were children. They never grew up in his eyes and they never grew up in their own eyes. He

made sure of that. They never left the farm. They of course got married but he handled all of their domestic matters except for the siring of his grandchildren. He never allowed them to discipline their own children. He took care of that for them. Her father thought of his father as another brother who was always trying to escape the never-relenting wrath of their grandfather.

2. He was smart, so he became a schoolteacher when he was eighteen and he left the farm which was an act of revolution against his grandfather who from that day forth considered him dead. He didn't want to end up like his father, hiding behind the barn. He taught school for three years in the Midwest and then he worked as an automobile salesman in the pioneer days of car selling.

3. There was an early marriage followed by an early divorce with feelings afterward that left the marriage hanging like a skeleton in her family's closet because he tried to keep it a secret. He probably had been very much in love.

4. There was a horrible automobile accident just before the First World War in which everybody was killed except him. It was one of those automobile accidents that leave deep spiritual scars like historical landmarks on the family and friends of the dead.

5. When America went into the First World War in 1917, he decided that he wanted to be a pilot, though he was in his late twenties. He was told that it would be impossible because he was too old but he projected so much energy into his desire to fly that he was accepted for pilot training and went to Florida and became a pilot.

In 1918 he went to France and flew a De Havilland and bombed a railroad station in France and one day he was flying over the German lines when little clouds began appearing around him and he thought that they were beautiful and flew for a long time before he realized that they were German antiaircraft guns trying to shoot him down.

Another time he was flying over France and a rainbow appeared behind the tail of his plane and every turn that the plane made, the rainbow also made the same turn and it followed after him through the skies of France for part of an afternoon in 1918.

6. When the war was over he got out a captain and he was travelling on a train through Texas when the middle-aged man sitting next to him and with whom he had been talking for about three hundred miles said, "If I was a young man like you and had a little extra cash, I'd go up to Idaho and start a bank. There's a good future in Idaho banking."

7. That's what her father did.

8. He went to Idaho and started a bank which soon led to three more banks and a large ranch. It was by now 1926 and everything was going all right.

9. He married a schoolteacher who was sixteen years his junior and for their honeymoon they took a train to Philadelphia and spent a week there.

10. When the stock market crashed in 1929 he was hit hard by it and had to give up his banks and a grocery store that he had picked up along the way, but he still had the ranch, though he had to put a mortgage on it.

11. He decided to go into sheep raising in 1931 and got a big flock and was very good to his sheepherders. He was so good to them that it was a subject of gossip in his part of Idaho. The sheep got some kind of horrible sheep disease and all died.

12. He got another big flock of sheep in 1933 and added more fuel to the gossip by continuing to be so good to his men. The sheep got some kind of horrible sheep disease and all died in 1934.

13. He gave his men a big bonus and went out of the sheep business.

14. He had just enough money left over after selling the ranch to pay off all his debts and buy a brand-new Chevrolet which he put his family into and he drove off to California to start all over again.

15. He was forty-four, had a twenty-eight-year-old wife and an infant daughter.

16. He didn't know anyone in California and it was the Depression.

17. His wife worked for a while in a prune shed and he parked cars at a lot in Hollywood.

18. He got a job as a bookkeeper for a small construction company.

19. His wife gave birth to a son.

20. In 1940 he went briefly into California real estate, but then decided not to pursue it any further and went back to work for the construction company as a bookkeeper.

21. His wife got a job as a checker in a grocery store where she worked for eight years and then an assistant manager quit and opened his own store and she went to work for him and she still works there.

22. She has worked twenty-three years now as a grocery checker for the same store.

23. She was very pretty until she was forty.

24. The construction company laid him off. They said he was too old to take care of the books. "It's time for you to go out to pasture," they joked. He was fifty-nine.

25. They rented the same house they lived in for twenty-five years, though they could have bought it at one time with no down payment and monthly payments of fifty dollars.

26. When his daughter was going to high school he was working there as the school janitor. She saw him in the halls. His working as a janitor was a subject that was very seldom discussed at home.

27. Her mother would make lunches for both of them.

28. He retired when he was sixty-five and became a very careful sweet wine alcoholic. He liked to drink whiskey but they couldn't afford to keep him in it. He stayed in the house most of the time and started drinking about ten o'clock, a few hours after his wife had gone off to work at the grocery store.

29. He would get quietly drunk during the course of the day. He always kept his wine bottles hidden in a kitchen cabinet and would secretly drink from them, though he was alone.

He very seldom made any bad scenes and the house was always clean when his wife got home from work. He did though after a while take on that meticulous manner of walking that alcoholics have when they are trying very carefully to act as if they aren't drunk.

30. He used sweet wine in place of life because he didn't have any more life to use.

31. He watched afternoon television.

32. Once he had been followed by a rainbow across the skies of France while flying a World War I airplane carrying bombs and machine guns.

33. "Your father died this afternoon."

JONATHAN STRONG
(1944–) WAS BORN IN
EVANSTON, ILLINOIS. HE
HAS BEEN DESCRIBED
AS "THE SALINGER OF
THE SIXTIES." HIS
BOOKS INCLUDE *TIKE
AND FIVE STORIES* AND
OURSELVES.

SAYIN
GOOD-BYE
TO TOM

Jonathan Strong

The two of us are walking down the wooden platform, Tom carryin his two suitcases an me carryin his duffel. There's the bus, so there's no sense in waitin around. The bus driver helps put the duffel an the suitcases in the luggage compartment an punches Tom's ticket. I haven't been thinkin about Tom's gettin on the bus an goin, but I know he's about to. We look at each other, and I make a funny face an he burps. We know each other's faces pretty well. Tom climbs on the bus. I want him to wait a minute, but he's already on an lookin out through the window. It's time to go. There's no sense in makin faces at each other till the bus leaves. I put my hand up meanin good-bye. Tom nods. I turn an walk up the platform by myself. Tom's probably watchin me go, but I don't turn around again.

The two of us are walkin down the wooden platform which has a sort of spring to it. I'm carryin Tom's duffel over my shoulder an then, when it gets too heavy, holdin it in front of me. The bus sticks out to the left from the end of the platform. Tom bumps his suitcases down the step an hands em to the driver who slides em in the luggage compartment. I stick one end of the duffel in, an the driver pushes it the rest of the way. Tom hands him his ticket which the driver punches an hands back. Then he goes back rearrangin the luggage, an Tom and I look at each other. We both feel funny sayin good-bye. We don't know whether to stand an talk a little more or just say good-bye an go off separately. Tom climbs on the bus. I guess he's too embarrassed standin around. I watch him for a few seconds in the bus window, takin off his jacket an sittin down. There are only a few other people inside the bus. I wave an turn to walk back to the station by myself feelin light without the duffel to carry.

We push through the station doors carryin all the luggage an walk down the platform to the bus. The boards feel warm an soft on my bare feet after the marble floor inside. Tom's wearin sandals which scuff along. He walks faster than I do, so I watch him from behind. He's tall and sloppy-lookin carryin his two suitcases. I look sort of closely at him cause I know I won't see him like this again. Next time we see each other won't be the same. I watch him puttin his stuff on the bus an showin his ticket. He's smilin an excited an bein very friendly to the bus driver. When he's about to get on we look at each other an realize it's time to go suddenly. I cross my eyes an stick out my front teeth. Tom lets out a huge burp, an I look around to see if the driver noticed, but he's busy with the luggage. Tom climbs on the bus. I don't feel like stayin around any longer, so I wave an head home.

ME: There it is.

TOM: Is that it?

ME: This is platform two. That's what they announced.

TOM: That's it then. What time is it?

ME: Don't know. You got time.

ME (*shifting duffel*): Hold it.

TOM: That's it, I can see the number.

ME: Hold it. Oh shit.

TOM: What's wrong?

ME: Nothin. Just adjustin this thing.

TOM: That's got all my books in it.

ME: You're tellin me!

TOM: Hope it's air-conditioned.

ME: They're all air-conditioned.

TOM (*to driver*): Is this the number twenty bus?

DRIVER: That's what she says.

TOM: You got room for all these?

DRIVER: Sure.

TOM: You about to leave soon?

DRIVER: Five minutes, son. Put that one in here. Fella, put that duffel there. Here, let me push it in. Got your tickets?

TOM: Here.

DRIVER: Just one of you fellas goin?

TOM: Yep, just me.

DRIVER (*punches ticket*): Here you are. Any seat.

TOM: Thanks. (*to me*) Hey, Mick, well, I guess I'll get on.

ME (*making cross-eyed face*): I guess so.

TOM: (*burps*)

ME: Holy shit! (*laughs*)

TOM: I'll write you.

ME: You better. Well, good-bye.

TOM: See you. (*climbs on*)

It's a hot night. The black gravel spreads around the place where the bus is at the end of the platform under the light. It's the only bus in the station. There's a fat lady lookin out one of the windows. After seein to his luggage and his ticket, Tom puts one foot up on the step of the bus. He's tall for the doorway, so he slouches down a bit an lets the other foot just hang in the air. He has on blue jeans an his sandals an a yellow shirt. He also left his blue jean jacket on, even though it's hot, so he wouldn't have to carry it in addition to the suitcases. He

118

pulls his hair back with his hand an looks at me. He's such a good-lookin guy. I'm embarrassed with him lookin at me, so I make a funny face. He makes a big juicy burp which he can do whenever he feels like it. Then he swings his body around sort of gracefully an climbs on the bus. I watch his flat bottom goin up the steps into the dark. I see him walkin down the aisle with his head bent forward. He takes off his jacket an slides himself over to a window near where I'm standin outside. His face is shadowy an handsome. It's the last way I see him, the way I'm goin to remember his face till I see him again. I walk back to the station an wonder if he's watchin me from the window, but I don't turn back.

Mick's helpin me carry my stuff down the platform to the bus. He's pokin along behind with the duffel which is pretty heavy. I should've let him carry the suitcases an carry the duffel myself, I guess. I hate leavin now. We got so close when we were high last night, ended up sort of fallin asleep together, it was beautiful, like kids. But it seemed funny this morning. We been nervous all day, not knowin how to say good-bye again after last night. It's goin to be hard. Look at that bus. I'll be on that thing for two solid days. Hope it's air-conditioned. Come on, Mick. Is he out of shape! I wish I was stayin around a little longer just to talk. We began to say some good things last night. What a sweaty guy that bus driver is! Here's the stuff. I don't suppose there's any sense in waitin around, might as well get on. There's that chipmunk face on Mick. You could be a handsome guy, Mick, if you didn't make that face. BURP! That was satisfyin. Well, there's no sense in standin around makin faces. Should we shake hands? No, I guess not. That's it, then. Up I go. This is not what I'd call air-conditioned. Boy, are you fat, lady. Here's a place. Take off the old jacket. Am I hot! Well, good-bye Mick, I'll miss you really a lot. You know it anyway. Standin in his cut-off jeans an T-shirt, barefoot, puttin his hand up, that's Mick. I won't see him again for a while. I'll remember him like that.

I'm walkin a few steps behind Tom down the platform. I drove him to the station an am helpin him carry his stuff. He won't be comin back for at least a year, and I don't know how it'll be without him around. I think of goin back to the room tonight an feelin pretty low cause he's gone. His bed'll be empty, an his stuff won't be there in the closet or the bathroom. Tom's walkin along thinkin of the trip, I guess. We talked last night how we would miss each other, and he had to admit he really would. I guess it was cause we were high, an it was on our minds. Last night we got into a lot of things we never got into before. He's a little nervous now. I'm standin behind him while he loads on his stuff an gets his ticket punched. My feet are black from the muddy gravel. It hurts em walkin on it. I step back up onto the platform an wipe my feet off with my hands. Tom's standin on the step of the bus. It's time to go. I make my cross-eyed chipmunk face, an Tom makes a beautiful burp. I laugh. That's it. He climbs on the bus. My stomach feels empty suddenly. I wish I had said good-bye more seriously. I wonder if he remembers what we talked about last night when we were high, how much us knowin each other an livin together has meant. Things are so split up, people don't get many real close friends. Everyone's always movin around.

Come through station doors.

Walk down platform, Tom ahead.

Me shift duffel.

Tom bump suitcases down step.

Give luggage to driver, driver punches ticket.

Me get up on platform, Tom start to get on bus.

Look at each other, me make face, Tom burp.

119

Say good-bye, Tom climb on bus.
Me wave, turn, walk back to station.
Tom in bus, probably watchin me go.

———————————

MAVIS GALLANT WAS BORN IN MONTREAL. SHE IS CONSIDERED TO BE A CANADIAN WRITER, ALTHOUGH SHE HAS LIVED MOST OF HER ADULT LIFE IN EUROPE. HER NOVELS AND SHORT FICTION FREQUENTLY DEAL WITH THE FOLLIES OF SELF-DELUSION. SHE IS OFTEN PRAISED FOR HER ACUTE PERCEPTIONS OF CHARACTER AND HER ABILITY TO WRITE DIALOGUE. HER MOST RECENT COLLECTION OF STORIES, *FROM THE FIFTEENTH DISTRICT,* APPEARED IN 1979.

THE PRODIGAL PARENT

Mavis Gallant

We sat on the screened porch of Rhoda's new house, which was close to the beach on the ocean side of Vancouver Island. I had come here in a straight line, from the East, and now that I could not go any farther without running my car into the sea, any consideration of wreckage and loss, or elegance of behavior, or debts owed (not of money, of my person) came to a halt. A conqueror in a worn blazer and a regimental tie, I sat facing my daughter, listening to her voice—now describing, now complaining—as if I had all the time in the world. Her glance drifted round the porch, which still contained packing cases. She could not do, or take in, a great deal at once. I have light eyes, like Rhoda's, but mine have been used for summing up.

Rhoda had bought this house and the cabins round it and a strip of maimed landscape with her divorce settlement. She hoped to make something out of the cabins, renting them weekends to respectable people who wanted a quiet place to drink. "Dune Vista" said a sign, waiting for someone to nail it to a tree. I wondered how I would fit in here—what she expected me to do. She still hadn't said. After the first formal Martinis she had made to mark my arrival, she began drinking rye, which she preferred. It was sweeter, less biting than the whiskey I remembered in my youth, and I wondered if my palate or its composition had changed. I started to say so, and my daughter said, "Oh, God, your accent again! You know what I thought you said now? 'Oxbow was a Cheswick charmer.'"

"No, no. Nothing like that."

"Try not sounding so British," she said.

"I don't, you know."

123

"Well, you don't sound Canadian."

The day ended suddenly, as if there had been a partial eclipse. In the new light I could see my daughter's face and hands.

"I guess I'm different from all my female relatives," she said. She had been comparing herself with her mother, and with half sisters she hardly knew. "I don't despise men, like Joanne does. There's always somebody. There's one now, in fact. I'll tell you about him. I'll tell you the whole thing, and you say what you think. It's a real mess. He's Irish, he's married, and he's got no money. Four children. He doesn't sleep with his wife."

"Surely there's an age limit for this?" I said. "By my count, you must be twenty-eight or -nine now."

"Don't I know it." She looked into the dark trees, darkened still more by the screens, and said without rancor, "It's not my fault. I wouldn't keep on falling for lushes and phonies if you hadn't been that way."

I put my glass down on the packing case she had pushed before me, and said, "I am not, I never was, and I never could be an alcoholic."

Rhoda seemed genuinely shocked. "I never said *that*. I never heard you had to be put in a hospital or anything, like my stepdaddy. But you used to stand me on a table when you had parties, Mother told me, and I used to dance to 'Piccolo Pete.' What happened to that record, I wonder? One of your wives most likely got it in lieu of alimony. But may God strike us both dead here and now if I ever said you were alcoholic." It must have been to her a harsh, clinical word, associated with straitjackets. "I'd like you to meet him," she said. "But I never know when he'll turn up. He's Harry Pay. The writer," she said, rather primly. "Somebody said he was a new-type Renaissance Man—I mean, he doesn't just sit around, he's a judo expert. He could throw *you* down in a second."

"Is he Japanese?"

"God, no. What makes you say that? I already told you what he is. He's white. Quite white, *entirely* white I mean."

"Well—I could hardly have guessed."

"You shouldn't have to guess," she said. "The name should be enough. He's famous. Round here, anyway."

"I'm sorry," I said. "I've been away so many years. Would you write the name down for me? So I can see how it's spelled?"

"I'll do better than that." It touched me to see the large girl she was suddenly moving so lightly. I heard her slamming doors in the living room behind me. She had been clumsy as a child, in every gesture like a wild creature caught. She came back to me with a dun folder out of which spilled loose pages, yellow and smudged. She thrust it at me and, as I groped for my spectacles, turned on an overhead light. "You read this," she said, "and I'll go make us some sandwiches, while I still can. Otherwise we'll break into another bottle and never eat anything. This is something he never shows *anyone*."

"It is my own life exactly," I said when she returned with the sandwiches, which she set awkwardly down. "At least, so far as school in England is concerned. Cold beds, cold food, cold lavatories. Odd that anyone still finds it interesting. There must be twenty written like it every year. The revolting school, the homosexual master, then a girl—saved!"

"Homo *what?*" said Rhoda, clawing the pages. "It's possible. He has a dirty mind, actually."

"Really? Has he ever asked you to do anything unpleasant, such as type his manuscripts?"

"Certainly not. He's got a perfectly good wife for that."

When I laughed, she looked indignant. She had given a serious answer to what she thought was a serious question. Our conversations were always like this — collisions.

"Well?" she said.

"Get rid of him."

She looked at me and sank down on the arm of my chair. I felt her breath on my face, light as a child's. She said, "I was waiting for something. I was waiting all day for you to say something personal, but I didn't think it would be that. Get rid of him? He's all I've got."

"All the more reason. You can do better."

"Who, for instance?" she said. "You? You're no use to me."

She had sent for me. I had come to Rhoda from her half sister Joanne, in Montreal. Joanne had repatriated me from Europe, with an air passage to back the claim. In a new bare apartment, she played severe sad music that was like herself. We ate at a scrubbed table the sort of food that can be picked up in the hand. She was the richest of my children, through her mother, but I recognized in her guarded, slanting looks the sort of avarice and fear I think of as a specific of women. One look seemed meant to tell me, "You waltzed off, old boy, but look at me now," though I could not believe she had wanted me only for that. "I'll never get married" was a remark that might have given me a lead. "I won't have anyone to lie to me, or make a fool of me, or spend my money for me." She waited to see what I would say. She had just come into this money.

"Feeling as you do, you probably shouldn't marry," I said. She looked at me as Rhoda was looking now. "Don't expect too much from men," I said.

"Oh, I don't!" she cried, so eagerly I knew she always would. The cheap sweet Ontario wine she favored and the smell of paint in her new rooms and the raw meals and incessant music combined to give me a violent attack of claustrophobia. It was probably the most important conversation we had.

"We can't have any more conversation now," said Rhoda. "Not after that. It's the end. You've queered it. I should have known. Well, eat your sandwiches now that I've made them."

"Would it seem petulant if, at this point, I did not eat a tomato sandwich?" I said.

"Don't be funny. I can't understand what you're saying anyway."

"If you don't mind, my dear," I said, "I'd rather be on my way."

"What do you mean, on your way? For one thing, you're in no condition to drive. Where d'you think you're going?"

"I can't very well go that way," I said, indicating the ocean I could not see. "I can't go back as I've come."

"It was a nutty thing, to come by car," she said. "It's not even all that cheap."

"As I can't go any farther," I said, "I shall stay. Not here, but perhaps not far."

"Doing what? What *can* you do? We've never been sure."

"I can get a white cane and walk the streets of towns. I can ask people to help me over busy intersections and then beg for money."

"You're kidding."

"I'm not. I shall say — let me think — I shall say I've had a mishap, lost my wallet, pension check not due for another week, postal strike delaying it even more — "

"That won't work. They'll send you to the welfare. You should see how we hand out welfare around here."

"I'm counting on seeing it," I said.

"You can't. It would look—" She narrowed her eyes and said, "If you're trying to shame me, forget it. Someone comes and says, 'That poor old blind bum says he's your father,' I'll just answer, 'Yes, what about it?'"

"My sight *is* failing, actually."

"There's welfare for that, too."

"We're at cross-purposes," I said. "I'm not looking for money."

"Then waja come here for?"

"Because Regan sent me on to Goneril, I suppose."

"That's a lie. Don't try to make yourself big. Nothing's ever happened to you."

"Well, in my uneventful life," I began, but my mind answered for me, "No, nothing." There are substitutes for incest but none whatever for love. What I needed now was someone who knew nothing about me and would never measure me against a promise or a past. I blamed myself, not for anything I had said but for having remembered too late what Rhoda was like. She was positively savage as an infant, though her school tamed her later on. I remember sitting opposite her when she was nine—she in an unbecoming tartan coat—while she slowly and seriously ate a large plate of ice cream. She was in London on a holiday with her mother, and as I happened to be there with my new family I gave her a day.

"Every Monday we have Thinking Day," she had said, of her school. "We think about the Brownies and the Baden-Powells and sometimes Jesus and all."

"Do you, really?"

"I can't *really*," Rhoda had said. "I never met any of them."

"Are you happy, at least?" I said, to justify my belief that no one was ever needed. But the savage little girl had become an extremely careful one.

That afternoon, at a matinée performance of "Peter Pan," I went to sleep. The slaughter of the pirates woke me, and as I turned, confident, expecting her to be rapt, I encountered a face of refusal. She tucked her lips in, folded her hands, and shrugged away when I helped her into a taxi.

"I'm sorry, I should not have slept in your company," I said. "It was impolite."

"It wasn't that," she burst out. "It was 'Peter Pan.' I hated it. It wasn't what I expected. You could see the wires. Mrs. Darling didn't look right. She didn't have a lovely dress on—only an old pink thing like a nightgown. Nana wasn't a real dog, it was a lady. I couldn't understand anything they said. Peter Pan wasn't a boy, he had bosoms."

"I noticed that, too," I said. "There must be a sound traditional reason for it. Perhaps Peter is really a mother figure."

"No, he's a *boy*."

I intercepted, again, a glance of stony denial—of me? We had scarcely met.

"I couldn't understand. They all had English accents," she complained.

For some reason that irritated me. "What the hell did you expect them to have?" I said.

"When I was little," said the nine-year-old, close to tears now, "I thought they were all Canadian."

The old car Joanne had given me was down on the beach, on the hard sand, with ribbons of tire tracks behind it as a sign of life, and my luggage locked inside. It had been there a few hours and already it looked abandoned—an old heap someone had left to rust among the lava rock. The sky was lighter than it had seemed from the porch. I picked up a sand dollar, chalky and white, with the tree of life on its underside, and as I slid it in my pocket, for luck, I felt between my fingers a rush of sand. I had spoken the truth, in part; the landscape through which I had recently travelled still shuddered before my eyes and I would not go back. I heard, then saw, Rhoda running down to where I stood. Her hair, which she wore gathered up in a bun, was half down, and she breathed, running, with her lips apart. For the first time I remembered something of the way she had seemed as a child, something more than an anecdote. She clutched my arm and said, "Why did you say I should ditch him? *Why?*"

I disengaged my arm, because she was hurting me, and said, "He can only give you bad habits."

"At my age?"

"Any age. Dissimulation. Voluntary barrenness—someone else has had his children. Playing house, a Peter-and-Wendy game, a life he would never dare try at home. There's the real meaning of Peter, by the way." But she had forgotten.

She clutched me again, to steady herself, and said, "I'm old enough to know everything. I'll soon be in my thirties. That's all I care to say."

It seemed to me I had only recently begun making grave mistakes. I had until now accepted all my children, regardless of who their mothers were. The immortality I had imagined had not been in them but on the faces of women in love. I saw, on the dark beach, Rhoda's mother, the soft hysterical girl whose fatal "I am pregnant" might have enmeshed me for life.

I said, "I wish they would find a substitute for immortality."

"I'm working on it," said Rhoda, grimly, seeming herself again. She let go my arm and watched me unlock the car door. "You'd have hated it here," she said, then, pleading, "You wouldn't want to live here like some charity case—have me support you?"

"I'd be enchanted," I said.

"No, no, you'd hate it," she said. "I couldn't look after you. I haven't got time. And you'd keep thinking I should do better than *him,* and the truth is I can't. You wouldn't want to end up like some old relation, fed in the kitchen and all."

"I don't know," I said. "It would be new."

"Oh," she cried, with what seemed unnecessary despair, "what did you come for? All right," she said. "I give up. You asked for it. You can stay. I mean, I'm inviting you. You can sit around and say, 'Oxbow was a Cheswick charmer,' all day and when someone says to me, 'Where jer father get his accent?' I'll say, 'It was a whole way of life.' But remember, you're not a prisoner or anything, around here. You can go whenever you don't like the food. I mean, if you don't like it, don't come to me and say, 'I don't like the food.' You're not my prisoner," she yelled, though her face was only a few inches from mine. "You're only my father. That's all you are."

WADE BELL IS A
SHORT-STORY WRITER
WHO NOW LIVES IN
CALGARY, ALBERTA.

1912:
THE BRIDGE
BEGINNING

Wade Bell

I think of the sun in our room.

That this room is green, a forest, grown thick of itself. It is a room, there is light and there is earth, wet, and leaves, alive to our turning. Green that is alive to light, turning, turned by the sun.

And outside, beyond the stand of poplar trees, the bridge, ugly and cold in the sun, half-built and ugly.

But this room, these plants that have grown because of her. They would not be, without her. Not here, not tame, in pots of her making and in wooden trays of mine: not in them, but somewhere, outside, they would be. Without her they would turn and grow, they would flower without her, and die.

It is a small house we live in, and we have one room of it only. It is a poor house, unlike others behind it that were built by men who have been here a decade or more and are becoming wealthy as the city grows.

This house, and our room in it, have what many rich men's houses do not have, and that is a view that other men think desirable. It is a view of the bridge, of the skeleton bridge thrust from the riverbank, partly made, already immense and to my mind ugly, already looking cold and ancient as if the winds of the North Saskatchewan had layered it with a century's grime and the northern clouds bathed it in sour rain. It is easy to imagine the bridge abandoned rather than new, to see it rotten and decaying above the spring colours of the valley.

This room is small and overfilled. It contains almost all we own. All, but for the cow and five of the chickens. This room contains a bed, which I have made, and its covers, which she has made. It contains two wood chairs which I have made and a small table, also of my making. These are crude and awkward furnishings as I have not the skill to make beauty, but they are sufficient, as are all our belongings. The room contains a daguerrotype of her mother and a painting of a cottage, a farm cottage that stands, in life, near the town of Falkirk in Scotland. It contains a washstand and a bowl and a pitcher. There is a cloth hanging from the edge of the washstand. There are curtains on the two windows. There are clothes hung on a rod beside the door and more clothes, a few, in a chest which I did not make but which was in this room when we came. There is little else. We take our meals with the landlord. The room is small and overfilled but we can be happy here, much of the time.

I watch my woman from the southern window as she milks the cow. She is large and not pretty but she works well and complains rarely. There is no luxury in her life, but there never has been and she is aware there never will. She has a way with animals and can make plants grow that would not grow for others. She is mainly cheerful and liked by people. She is barren and although this troubles her it matters little to me, for I have children elsewhere. She says she is content not to marry but I know she is not content and I would likely have married her had I been free to do so, but I am not and she knows it. We do not talk about that. She says she is content to be at home, in this small room, and to tend the chickens and the cow. She has had enough hard work in her lifetime, both here and where she came from.

She seems content, but I am not. The full realization of that has come only now, sitting in the sun and green warmth of this too small room. I watch her rise with a small pail of milk, turn to talk with a neighbour woman. No, I am not content. I grasp that truth now: I am not content and must think of leaving. It has nothing to do with her although I will not take her with me when I leave. She is a good woman and she should marry. She must find a widower with children and these she should raise and make flower like the plants in this room. She is a good woman and it will not be because of her that I leave.

It is the bridge. It is the ugliness of the bridge that I am seeing today and it is the fear of it that has erupted in my mind this day. It is because of Campbell that I will leave. It was only a few hours ago that we were let off work although it seems like it has been days. We were let off in the middle of the afternoon because of Campbell. Because of him and because of this afternoon I will leave. His life was not worth the bridge, nor is mine. I realize that now. It is the bridge and it is Campbell's dying. It is the bridge and Campbell's death that make me go. I know that now. I am afraid to die.

The bridge could give me work for many months. After it is built I could find an easy job here in this city and this room could be my home and the woman my woman, and we could sit in the evenings and watch the heavy engines cross the bridge and watch the river flow beneath it. We could live here and die in our time. I could do this but I will not. I will leave. It is not the whisky I have had this afternoon that has made me afraid, but it is the whisky that shows me my fear in this vision of another man falling. Campbell fell this afternoon and Campbell falls now, over and over his body is falling, falling and falling without end or so it seems but it does end although I did not then and do not now see his body land as it landed among trees. But I see him falling. I do not have to close my eyes to see him. I see him begin to fall.

It was as if he stumbled, as if he merely lost his balance as we all can lose our balance, even as an animal will sometimes lose its balance and if not fall at least stumble and begin to turn and feel the beginnings of helplessness before righting itself. He had looked up into the sun that burnt from the southwest and as he looked into the sun he went to move along the beam we were both on. It was as if he stumbled. He did not right himself as an animal might. He merely looked surprised that his foot had not landed on steel but dangled in air and his surprise must have been mirrored in my eyes as he looked at me as if to say I have lost my balance. There was only surprise then in his face but that changed to fear and then panic, the panic coming into him slowly, it seemed, as his arm went up and found nothing to hold to, the panic covering his face and his eyes still looking at me, it happening so slowly, so slowly, it all happening there so close to me, his arms and legs stretching to feel something but feeling nothing, his eyes widening and his body floating out and down and then only down and me watching him fall, unable to look away, not even seeing what was beyond him and below him, only him, only Campbell suddenly disappearing in the green soft garden of leaves very far below near the edge of the river, directly below me. I watched him fall and now I am afraid. It is time for me to leave.

MADELEINE FERRON IS
THE SISTER OF AUTHOR
JACQUES FERRON. SHE
HAS PUBLISHED TWO
SHORT-STORY
COLLECTIONS. "BE
FRUITFUL AND
MULTIPLY" IS TAKEN
FROM HER COLLECTION
COEUR DE SUCRE.
FERRON, LIKE HER
BROTHER, WRITES
OFTEN OF LIFE IN
SMALL-TOWN QUEBEC
AND IS NOTED FOR HER
CLEAR, OFTEN IRONIC
STYLE.

BE
FRUITFUL
AND
MULTIPLY

Madeleine Ferron

Translated by Sheila Watson

About eight o'clock they woke with a start. Amazed and confused, she shrank from the unexpectedness of her waking. She wasn't dreaming. It was true. She had been married the day before and was waking up with her husband in a bed in the neighbour's house. He was pushing back his hair and swearing as he painfully lifted his head. He had gone to bed dead drunk. "You cannot refuse," they said. "After all, you are the bridegroom."

Half way through the evening he was drunk already and a shock of brown hair had fallen forward over his face without his making any effort at all to throw it back with a shake of his head as he usually did. Shifting from leg to leg, her senses blunted with sleep, she watched, heavy-eyed, the progress of the festivity, diverted from time to time by the almost wild pleasure he was taking in his own wedding feast.

Since it was her wedding too, she resolutely stayed awake, all the while envying her cousin who slept peacefully, her head against the corner of the wall. They were the same age—thirteen-and-a-half. At that age sleep could be pardoned, she had heard them say again and again. Of course, but not on the night of one's wedding.

It was long after midnight when at last he signalled her to follow him. They went through the garden so that no one could see them or play mean tricks on them. She helped him to jump over the fence, to cross the ditch, and to climb the stairs. He fell across the bed and began to snore at once, his hands clenched like a child's. He was eighteen. She slept, curled round on an empty corner of the mattress.

They got up quickly as soon as they woke, ashamed to have stayed in bed so long. He ran to hitch up a buggy which he drove around in front of his in-laws' house. His wife's trunk was loaded on and he helped her up. He was formal, embarrassed; she, almost joyful. Then he turned the horse at a trot towards the property that had been prepared for them. He was to be the second neighbour down the road. She waved happily again and again and her mother, who was crying, kept watching, until they had rounded the corner, the blond braid that swung like a pendulum over the back of the buggy seat.

All day they worked eagerly getting settled. In the evening they went to bed early. He embraced her eagerly. Face to face with a heat that flamed and entangled her in its curious movement, she was frightened.

"What are you doing?" she asked.

He answered quietly, "You are the sheep and I am the ram."

"Oh," she said. It was simple when one had a reference point.

On the first mornings of their life together, after he had left for the fields, she ran quickly to her mother's.

"Are you managing?" her mother always asked.

"Yes," the child replied smiling.

"Your husband, is he good to you?"

"Oh yes," she said. "He says I am a pretty sheep."

Sheep... sheep. The mother, fascinated, watched her daughter attentively but did not dare to question her further.

"Go back to your husband now," she said. "Busy yourself about the house and get his meal ready."

Since the girl hesitated uncertainly as if she did not understand, her mother sprinkled sugar on a slice of bread spread with cream, gave it to her and pushed her gently toward the door. The child went down the road eating her bread and the mother, reassured, leaned sadly against the wall of the house watching the thick swaying braid until the girl turned the corner of the road.

Little by little the young wife spaced her visits. In autumn when the cold rain began to fall, she came only on Sundays. She had found her own rhythm. Was she too eager, too ambitious? Perhaps she was simply inattentive. Her tempo was too swift. She always hurried now. She wove more bed covers than her chest could hold, cultivated more vegetables than they could eat, raised more calves than they knew how to sell.

And the children came quickly — almost faster than nature permits. She was never seen without a child in her arms, one in her belly, and another at her heels. She raised them well, mechanically, without counting them; accepted them as the seasons are accepted; watched them leave, not with fatalism or resignation but steadfast and untroubled, face to face with the ineluctable cycle that makes the apple fall when it is ripe.

The simple mechanism she had set in motion did not falter. She was the cog wheel that had no right to oversee the whole machine. Everything went well. Only the rhythm was too fast. She outstripped the seasons. The begetting of her children pressed unreasonably on that of her grandchildren and the order was broken. Her daughters and her sons already had many children when she was still bearing others — giving her grandsons uncles who were younger than they were and for whom they could have no respect.

She had twenty-two children. It was extravagant. Fortunately, as one child was carried in the front door, beribboned and wailing, one went out the rear door alone, its knapsack on its back. Nevertheless, it was extravagant. She never realized it.

When her husband was buried and her youngest son married, she caught her breath, decided finally on slippers and a rocking chair. The mechanism could not adjust to a new rhythm. It broke down. She found herself disoriented, incapable of directing the stranger she had become, whom she did not know, who turned round and round with outstretched arms, more and more agitated.

"And if I should visit my family?" she asked her neighbour one day. She had children settled in the four corners of the province, some even exiled to the United States. She would go to take the census or, rather, she would go like a bishop to make the rounds of the diocese.

She had been seen leaving one morning, walking slowly. She had climbed into the bus, a small black cardboard suitcase in her hand. She had smiled at her neighbours but her eyes were still haggard.

She went first to the States. She was introduced to the wife of her grandson who spoke no French and to all the others whom she looked at searchingly.

"That one," she said, "is she my child or my child's child?"

The generations had become confused. She no longer knew.

She went back to Sept-Isles. One day, when she was rocking on the veranda with one of her sons, he pointed out a big dark-haired young man who was coming down the street.

"Look, mother," her son said. "He is my youngest." He was eighteen and a shock of hair fell forward over his face. She began to cry.

"It is he," she said. "It is my husband."

The next day she was taken to the home of one of her daughters, whom she called by her sister's name. Her daughter took care of her for several days and then took her to the house of the other daughter who, after much kindness, took her to the home of one of the oldest of the grandsons. She asked no questions. She cried.

Finally, one of her boys, chaplain in a home for the aged, came to get her. She followed him obediently. When he presented her to the assembled community, she turned to him and said quietly, "Tell me, are all these your brothers?"

PART FOUR
THE USE OF FORCE

◆

137

WILLIAM CARLOS
WILLIAMS (1883 – 1963)
WAS BORN IN
RUTHERFORD, NEW
JERSEY. BETTER KNOWN
AS A POET THAN A
SHORT-STORY WRITER,
WILLIAMS PRACTISED
MEDICINE IN
RUTHERFORD ALL HIS
LIFE. HIS BEST-KNOWN
POEM IS THE MAJOR
WORK *PATERSON*.

THE USE OF FORCE

FORCE

William Carlos Williams

They were new patients to me, all I had was the name, Olson. Please come down as soon as you can, my daughter is very sick.

When I arrived I was met by the mother, a big startled looking woman, very clean and apologetic who merely said, Is this the doctor? and let me in. In the back, she added. You must excuse us, doctor, we have her in the kitchen where it is warm. It is very damp here sometimes.

The child was fully dressed and sitting on her father's lap near the kitchen table. He tried to get up, but I motioned for him not to bother, took off my overcoat and started to look things over. I could see that they were all very nervous, eyeing me up and down distrustfully. As often, in such cases, they weren't telling me more than they had to, it was up to me to tell them; that's why they were spending three dollars on me.

The child was fairly eating me up with her cold, steady eyes, and no expression to her face whatever. She did not move and seemed, inwardly, quiet; an unusually attractive little thing, and as strong as a heifer in appearance. But her face was flushed, she was breathing rapidly, and I realized that she had a high fever. She had magnificent blonde hair, in profusion. One of those picture children often reproduced in advertising leaflets and the photogravure sections of the Sunday papers.

She's had a fever for three days, began the father and we don't know what it comes from. My wife has given her things, you know, like people do, but it don't do no good. And there's been a lot of sickness around. So we tho't you'd better look her over and tell us what is the matter.

As doctors often do I took a trial shot at it as a point of departure. Has she had a sore throat?

Both parents answered me together, No...No, she says her throat don't hurt her.

Does your throat hurt you? added the mother to the child. But the little girl's expression didn't change nor did she move her eyes from my face.

Have you looked?

I tried to, said the mother, but I couldn't see.

As it happens we had been having a number of cases of diphtheria in the school to which this child went during that month and we were all, quite apparently, thinking of that, though no one had as yet spoken of the thing.

Well, I said, suppose we take a look at the throat first. I smiled in my best professional manner and asking for the child's first name I said, come on, Mathilda, open your mouth and let's take a look at your throat.

Nothing doing.

Aw, come on, I coaxed, just open your mouth wide and let me take a look. Look, I said opening both hands wide. I haven't anything in my hands. Just open up and let me see.

Such a nice man, put in the mother. Look how kind he is to you. Come on, do what he tells you to. He won't hurt you.

At that I ground my teeth in disgust. If only they wouldn't use the word "hurt" I might be able to get somewhere. But I did not allow myself to be hurried or disturbed but speaking quietly and slowly I approached the child again.

As I moved my chair a little nearer suddenly with one cat-like movement both her hands clawed instinctively for my eyes and she almost reached them too. In fact she knocked my glasses flying and they fell, though unbroken, several feet away from me on the kitchen floor.

Both the mother and father almost turned themselves inside out in embarrassment and apology. You bad girl, said the mother, taking her and shaking her by one arm. Look what you've done. The nice man...

For heaven's sake, I broke in. Don't call me a nice man to her. I'm here to look at her throat on the chance that she might have diphtheria and possibly die of it. But that's nothing to her. Look here, I said to the child, we're going to look at your throat. You're old enough to understand what I'm saying. Will you open it now by yourself or shall we have to open it for you?

Not a move. Even her expression hadn't changed. Her breaths however were coming faster and faster. Then the battle began. I had to do it. I had to have a throat culture for her own protection. But first I told the parents that it was entirely up to them. I explained the danger but said that I would not insist on a throat examination so long as they would take the responsibility.

If you don't do what the doctor says you'll have to go to the hospital, the mother admonished her severely.

Oh yeah? I had to smile to myself. After all, I had already fallen in love with the savage brat, the parents were contemptible to me. In the ensuing struggle they grew more and more abject, crushed, exhausted while she surely rose to magnificent heights of insane fury of effort bred of her terror of me.

The father tried his best, and he was a big man but the fact that she was his daughter, his shame at her behavior and his dread of hurting her made him release her just at the critical moment several times when I had almost achieved success, till I wanted to kill him. But his dread also that she might have diphtheria made him tell me to go on, go on though he himself was almost

140

fainting, while the mother moved back and forth behind us raising and lowering her hands in an agony of apprehension.

Put her in front of you on your lap, I ordered, and hold both her wrists.

But as soon as he did the child let out a scream. Don't, you're hurting me. Let go of my hands. Let them go I tell you. Then she shrieked terrifyingly, hysterically. Stop it! Stop it! You're killing me!

Do you think she can stand it, doctor! said the mother.

You get out, said the husband to his wife. Do you want her to die of diphtheria?

Come on now, hold her, I said.

Then I grasped the child's head with my left hand and tried to get the wooden tongue depressor between her teeth. She fought, with clenched teeth, desperately! But now I also had grown furious—at a child. I tried to hold myself down but I couldn't. I know how to expose a throat for inspection. And I did my best. When finally I got the wooden spatula behind the last teeth and just the point of it into the mouth cavity, she opened up for an instant but before I could see anything she came down again and gripping the wooden blade between her molars she reduced it to splinters before I could get it out again.

Aren't you ashamed, the mother yelled at her. Aren't you ashamed to act like that in front of the doctor?

Get me a smooth-handled spoon of some sort, I told the mother. We're going through with this. The child's mouth was already bleeding. Her tongue was cut and she was screaming in wild hysterical shrieks. Perhaps I should have desisted and come back in an hour or more. No doubt it would have been better. But I have seen at least two children lying dead in bed of neglect in such cases, and feeling that I must get a diagnosis now or never I went at it again. But the worst of it was that I too had got beyond reason. I could have torn the child apart in my own fury and enjoyed it. It was a pleasure to attack her. My face was burning with it.

The damned little brat must be protected against her own idiocy, one says to one's self at such times. Others must be protected against her. It is social necessity. And all these things are true. But a blind fury, a feeling of adult shame, bred of a longing for muscular release are the operatives. One goes on to the end.

In a final unreasoning assault I overpowered the child's neck and jaws. I forced the heavy silver spoon back of her teeth and down her throat till she gagged. And there it was—both tonsils covered with membrane. She had fought valiantly to keep me from knowing her secret. She had been hiding that sore throat for three days at least and lying to her parents in order to escape just such an outcome as this.

Now truly she *was* furious. She had been on the defensive before but now she attacked. Tried to get off her father's lap and fly at me while tears of defeat blinded her eyes.

RANDY BROWN IS A
TORONTO WRITER BEST
KNOWN FOR HIS SHORT
STORY, "HEIL!"

142

HEIL!

[handwritten: →HITLER WAS CALLED THIS]

Randy Brown *[handwritten: Life unpredictable]*

[handwritten: ATmosphere Imp. recognizable situation]

Bob woke up and listened. He turned to his wife, Carol, but she was still breathing heavily into her pillow. He swung his feet out of bed and walked over to the window. There, standing on the porch below, illuminated by the backdoor light, was a man. He was beckoning to him. Bob bent over and stared. *[handwritten: when someone's strange we tend to stare at them]* The man seemed to know he was there, for he beckoned even more insistently.

"Carol!" said Bob. She rolled over and raised her head. "There's someone out there, someone's standing on the porch."

Carol lifted herself up on her hands.

"What does he want?" she said.

"I don't know. He seems to be waving at me."

Carol came over beside him.

"Oh, my God!"

"What's the matter?"

"Look at him," replied Carol. Then Bob realized. The man wore only a bathrobe over his pajamas and was in his bare feet. *[handwritten: bum]* Six inches of snow lay on the ground. Carol clutched his arm. "Don't let him in."

Bob hesitated. It seemed incongruous. Where could he have come from? Their farmhouse was half a mile from the road and a mile from the next house. They spent only occasional weekends there during the winter so it didn't seem possible that a neighbor would come that way for help. Yet a half-dressed man was standing on their porch, freezing to death, beckoning. *[handwritten: loss / are]*

[handwritten: scary] "I've got to let him in, Carol," he blurted.

"No, no, don't. He looks too strange. Call the police." *[handwritten: PARANOIED]*

[handwritten: we should be]

[handwritten: compassion vs. paranoya.]

143

"I've got to let him in. He'd be dead by the time the police got here. Anyway, he's alone. I can handle one man."

"I won't let you! I won't let you! Call the police, oh please, call the police!"

"You stay here," he ordered and started out of the room.

"No! Don't leave me here alone! I'll come with you." ?PANIC

"O.K. Suit yourself, but come on."

Bob turned on the hall lights and headed downstairs to the kitchen with Carol right behind. They could hear the man pounding on the door, a loud, almost panic-stricken sound.

"O.K., O.K., I'm coming!"

PARANOIA "Wait!" called Carol. She pulled open the utensil drawer and lifted out the carving knife. Bob turned. Her hands shook so that she nearly dropped it on the floor.

"Just leave that on the table," he said. The pounding on the door was deafening. Bob hesitated. He could not understand the situation. They led such an ordered life. He had never come across anything that so defied an explanation. Carol had retreated into the far corner of the kitchen, her eyes fixed on him, and between them, on the table, lay the knife, shiny and ominous. He knew he could never use it. Shaking his head, he crossed to the door and pulled back the latch.

he does *use* of ← -self defense

The door burst open and the man was on him, pinning his arms to his sides. They crashed to the floor and Bob struggled for his breath amidst the shock of the impact and Carol's piercing scream. He kicked out and the kitchen table went crashing over. Carol's screams faded into the background of his own rasping breath as he struggled to beat the man off. The knife was on the floor only a foot away. He lunged to grasp it and stabbed it into the man's back again and again.

Bob rolled from under the body.

"It's all right," he gasped, staggering up, "It's all right." Carol kept screaming. Following the line of her gaze, he turned around. The back door was crowded with a dozen more of the same men, all in pajamas and bare feet, all babbling and shoving their way into the house.

Bob swung the knife at the figures that seemed only a blur to him. Carol was lifted up bodily and thrown down, her screams stifled. The press of the men forced Bob back into the corner. He could not advance against them. One large figure came out of the blur and Bob stabbed the knife deep into the man's chest. The figure toppled over onto him and he threw it back into the arms grasping at him. Directly behind him was the open cellar door. He darted through and slammed it, then quickly jammed several timbers against it so that it was immovable. The men tried to knock it down, but they could not, and they finally left it alone.

refuge/protection/Assylum/shelter

IRONIC For several hours Bob crouched alone in his sanctuary, listening. He could hear Carol. She tried to scream quite often. Bob thought she couldn't scream because she couldn't get her breath. Mostly, she groaned. At the first she managed to scream about once every five minutes, but after about an hour, she moaned. There were other noises, too, of furniture being pulled over and general destruction going on, but he barely registered those noises. It was Carol he was listening for, and when they threw her around, he knew, because the sound of her body was softer than that of the furniture. He prayed that she would die. He began to curse her, screaming at her to die. Several times he caught himself screaming at the top of his lungs. "Die, die, die, die!"

he helpless. becomes insane couldn't do anything

In the morning, when the search parties arrived, they found Carol's naked, frozen body by the front steps. The madmen were still roaming about the house.

144

They led an ordered life. ignores all matter (madness) in world ⇒ like the SP. INATIES

The police loaded them into several paddy wagons. They broke down the cellar door. Bob was sitting on the top step, babbling gently to himself and playing with the drawstring of his pajamas.

"I don't know how this one got down here," said the officer, "but take him and throw him into the wagon with the others."

Real horrew;

Names Bob & Carol are known names don't think anything will happen

Symbolic of madness of what's going on around us.

Affraid of approaching someone.

STORY is about Bob.
pattern - no foreshadowing
Setting - part of The horror.
Madman → symbolic of what's going out in world
Atmosphere → fear & tension, compassion, paranoya.

title defines story of madness outside,
THEME:
— we live in our own worlds & ignore kaos around us.

STEPHEN CRANE (1871 –
1900) WAS BORN IN
NEWARK, NEW JERSEY.
HIS STORIES AND
NOVELS INTRODUCED
AN UNCOMPROMISING
REALISM INTO
AMERICAN
LITERATURE. CRANE'S
BEST-KNOWN BOOK IS
*THE RED BADGE OF
COURAGE: AN EPISODE
OF THE AMERICAN
CIVIL WAR* (1895).

THE UPTURNED FACE

Stephen Crane

What will we do now?" said the adjutant, troubled and excited.

"Bury him" said Timothy Lean.

The two officers looked down close to their toes where lay the body of their comrade. The face was chalk-blue; gleaming eyes stared at the sky. Over the two upright figures was a windy sound of bullets, and on top of the hill Lean's prostrate company of Spitzbergen infantry was firing measured volleys.

"Don't you think it would be better—" began the adjutant. "We might leave him until tomorrow."

"No," said Lean. "I can't hold that post an hour longer. I've got to fall back, and we've got to bury old Bill."

"Of course," said the adjutant, at once. "Your men got entrenching tools?"

Lean shouted back to his little line, and two men came slowly, one with a pick, one with a shovel. They started in the direction of the Rostina sharpshooters. Bullets cracked near their ears. "Dig here," said Lean gruffly. The men, thus caused to lower their glances to the turf, became hurried and frightened, merely because they could not look to see whence the bullets came. The dull beat of the pick striking the earth sounded amid the swift snap of close bullets. Presently the other private began to shovel.

"I suppose," said the adjutant slowly, "we'd better search his clothes for— things."

Lean nodded. Together in curious abstraction they looked at the body. Then Lean stirred his shoulders suddenly, arousing himself.

"Yes," he said, "we'd better see what he's got." He dropped to his knee, and his hands approached the body of the dead officer. But his hands wavered over the buttons of the tunic. The first button was brick-red with drying blood, and he did not seem to dare to touch it.

"Go on," said the adjutant, hoarsely.

Lean stretched his wooden hand, and his fingers fumbled the bloodstained buttons. At last he rose with ghastly face. He had gathered a watch, a whistle, a pipe, a tobacco-pouch, a handkerchief, a little case of cards and papers. He looked at the adjutant. There was a silence. The adjutant was feeling that he had been a coward to make Lean do all the grisly business.

"Well," said Lean, "that's all, I think. You have his sword and revolver?"

"Yes," said the adjutant, his face working, and then he burst out in a sudden strange fury at the two privates. "Why don't you hurry up with that grave? What are you doing, anyhow? Hurry, do you hear? I never saw such stupid—"

Even as he cried out in his passion, the two men were labouring for their lives. Ever overhead the bullets were spitting.

The grave was finished. It was not a masterpiece—a poor little shallow thing. Lean and the adjutant again looked at each other in a curious silent communication.

Suddenly the adjutant croaked out a weird laugh. It was a terrible laugh which had its origin in that part of the mind which is first moved by the singing of the nerves. "Well," he said humorously to Lean, "I suppose we had best tumble him in."

"Yes," said Lean. The two privates stood waiting, bent over their implements. "I suppose," said Lean, "it would be better if we laid him in ourselves."

"Yes," said the adjutant. Then, apparently remembering that he had made Lean search the body, he stooped with great fortitude and took hold of the dead officer's clothing. Lean joined him. Both were particular that their fingers should not feel the corpse. They tugged away; the corpse lifted, heaved, toppled, flopped into the grave, and the two officers, straightening, looked again at each other—they were always looking at each other. They sighed with relief.

The adjutant said, "I suppose we should—we should say something. Do you know the service, Tim?"

"They don't read the service until the grave is filled in," said Lean, pressing his lips to an academic expression.

"Don't they?" said the adjutant, shocked that he had made the mistake. "Oh, well," he cried, suddenly, "let us—let us say something—while he can hear us."

"All right," said Lean. "Do you know the service?"

"I can't remember a line of it," said the adjutant.

Lean was extremely dubious. "I can repeat two lines, but—"

"Well, do it," said the adjutant. "Go as far as you can. That's better than nothing. And the beasts have got our range exactly."

Lean looked at his two men. "Attention," he barked. The privates came to attention with a click, looking much aggrieved. The adjutant lowered his helmet to his knee. Lean, bareheaded, stood over the grave. The Rostina sharpshooters fired briskly.

"O Father, our friend has sunk in the deep waters of death, but his spirit has leaped toward Thee as the bubble arises from the lips of the drowning. Perceive, we beseech, O Father, the little flying bubble, and—"

Lean, although husky and ashamed, had suffered no hesitation up to this point, but he stopped with a hopeless feeling and looked at the corpse.

The adjutant moved uneasily. "And from Thy superb heights," he began, and then he too came to an end.

148

"And from Thy superb heights," said Lean.

The adjutant suddenly remembered a phrase in the back of the Spitzbergen burial service, and he exploited it with the triumphant manner of a man who has recalled everything, and can go on.

"O God, have mercy—"

"O God, have mercy—"said Lean.

"Mercy," repeated the adjutant, in quick failure.

"Mercy," said Lean. And then he was moved by some violence of feeling, for he turned upon his two men and tigerishly said, "Throw the dirt in."

The fire of the Rostina sharpshooters was accurate and continuous.

One of the aggrieved privates came forward with his shovel. He lifted his first shovel-load of earth, and for a moment of inexplicable hesitation it was held poised above this corpse which from its chalk-blue face looked keenly out from the grave. Then the soldier emptied his shovel on—on the feet.

Timothy Lean felt as if tons had been swiftly lifted from off his forehead. He had felt that perhaps the private might empty the shovel on—on the face. It had been emptied on the feet. There was a great point gained there—ha, ha!—the first shovelful had been emptied on the feet. How satisfactory!

The adjutant began to babble. "Well, of course—a man we've messed with all these years—impossible—you can't, you know, leave your intimate friends rotting on the field. Go on, for God's sake, and shovel, you."

The man with the shovel suddenly ducked, grabbed his left arm with his right hand, and looked at his officer for orders. Lean picked the shovel from the ground. "Go to the rear," he said to the wounded man. He also addressed the other private. "You get under cover, too; I'll finish this business."

The wounded man scrambled hard for the top of the ridge without devoting any glances to the direction from whence the bullets came, and the other man followed at an equal pace; but he was different, in that he looked back anxiously three times.

This is merely the way—often—of the hit and the unhit.

Timothy Lean filled the shovel, hesitated, and then, in a movement which was like a gesture of abhorrence, he flung the dirt into the grave, and as it landed it made a sound—plop. Lean suddenly stopped and mopped his brow—a tired labourer.

"Perhaps we have been wrong," said the adjutant. His glance wavered stupidly. "It might have been better if we hadn't buried him just at this time. Of course, if we advance tomorrow the body would have been—"

"Damn you," said Lean, "shut your mouth." He was not the senior officer.

He again filled the shovel and flung the earth. Always the earth made that sound—plop. For a space, Lean worked frantically, like a man digging himself out of danger.

Soon there was nothing to be seen but the chalk-blue face. Lean filled the shovel. "Good God," he cried to the adjutant. "Why didn't you turn him somehow when you put him in? This—" Then Lean began to stutter.

The adjutant understood. He was pale to the lips. "Go on, man," he cried, beseechingly, almost in a shout.

Lean swung back the shovel. It went forward in a pendulum curve. When the earth landed it made a sound—plop.

OCTAVIO PAZ (1914–)
WAS BORN IN MEXICO.
PAZ HAS SPENT A
LIFETIME IN WRITING,
TEACHING, AND
DIPLOMATIC WORK. HIS
PUBLICATIONS INCLUDE
*LABYRINTH OF
SOLITUDE,
ALTERNATING
CURRENT,* AND *THE
SIREN AND THE
SEASHELL.*

THE BLUE BOUQUET

Octavio Paz

Translated by Lysander Kemp

When I woke up I was soaked with sweat. The floor of my room had been freshly sprinkled and a warm vapor was rising from the red tiles. A moth flew around and around the naked bulb, dazzled by the light. I got out of the hammock and walked barefoot across the room, being careful not to step on a scorpion if one had come out of its hiding place to enjoy the coolness of the floor. I stood at the window for a few minutes, breathing in the air from the fields and listening to the vast, feminine breathing of the night. Then I walked over to the washstand, poured some water into the enamel basin, and moistened a towel. I rubbed my chest and legs with the damp cloth, dried myself a little, and got dressed, first making sure that no bugs had got into the seams of my clothes. I went leaping down the green-painted staircase and blundered into the hotelkeeper at the door. He was blind in one eye, a glum and reticent man, sitting there in a rush chair, smoking a cigarette, with his eyes half closed.

Now he peered at me with his good eye. "Where are you going, señor?" he asked in a hoarse voice.

"To take a walk. It's too hot to stay in my room."

"But everything's closed up by now. And we don't have any streetlights here. You'd better stay in."

I shrugged my shoulders, mumbled, "I'll be right back," and went out into the darkness. At first I couldn't see anything at all. I groped my way along the stone-paved street. I lit a cigarette. Suddenly the moon came out from behind a black cloud, lighting up a weather-beaten white wall. I stopped in my tracks, blinded by that whiteness. A faint breeze stirred the air and I could smell the fragrance of the tamarind trees. The night was murmurous with the sounds of leaves and insects. The crickets had bivouacked among the tall weeds. I raised my eyes: up there the stars were also camping out. I thought that the whole universe was a grand system of signals, a conversation among enormous beings. My own actions, the creak of a cricket, the blinking of a star, were merely pauses and syllables, odd fragments of that dialogue. I was only one syllable, of only one word. But what was that word? Who was uttering it? And to whom? I tossed my cigarette onto the sidewalk. It fell in a glowing arc, giving off sparks like a miniature comet.

I walked on, slowly, for a long while. I felt safe and free, because those great lips were pronouncing me so clearly, so joyously. The night was a garden of eyes.

Then when I was crossing a street I could tell that someone had come out of a doorway. I turned around but couldn't see anything. I began to walk faster. A moment later I could hear the scuff of huaraches on the warm stones. I didn't want to look back, even though I knew the shadow was catching up with me. I tried to run. I couldn't. Then I stopped short. And before I could defend myself I felt the point of a knife against my back, and a soft voice said, "Don't move señor, or you're dead."

Without turning my head I asked, "What do you want?"

"Your eyes, señor." His voice was strangely gentle, almost embarrassed.

"My eyes? What are you going to do with my eyes? Look, I've got a little money on me. Not much, but it's something. I'll give you everything I've got if you'll let me go. Don't kill me."

"You shouldn't be scared, señor. I'm not going to kill you. I just want your eyes."

"But what do you want them for?"

"It's my sweetheart's idea. She'd like to have a bouquet of blue eyes. There aren't many people around here that have them."

"Mine won't do you any good. They aren't blue, they're light brown."

"No, señor. Don't try to fool me. I know they're blue."

"But we're both Christians, hombre! You can't just gouge my eyes out. I'll give you everything I've got on me."

"Don't be so squeamish." His voice was harsh now. "Turn around."

I turned around. He was short and slight, with a palm sombrero half covering his face. He had a long machete in his right hand. It glittered in the moonlight.

"Hold a match to your face."

I lit a match and held it up in front of my face. The flame made me close my eyes and he pried up my lids with his fingers. He couldn't see well enough, so he stood on tiptoes and stared at me. The match burned my fingers and I threw it away. He was silent for a moment.

"Aren't you sure now? They aren't blue."

"You're very clever, señor," he said. "Light another match."

I lit another and held it close to my eyes. He tugged at my sleeve. "Kneel down."

I knelt. He grabbed my hair and bent my head back. Then he leaned over me, gazing intently, and the machete came closer and closer till it touched my eyelids. I shut my eyes.

"Open them up," he told me. "Wide."

I opened my eyes again. The match-flame singed my lashes.

Suddenly he let go. "No. They're not blue. Excuse me." And he disappeared.

I huddled against the wall with my hands over my face. Later I got up and ran

152

through the deserted streets for almost an hour. When I finally stumbled into the plaza I saw the hotelkeeper still sitting at the door. I went in without speaking to him. The next day I got out of that village.

GEORG HEYM (1887 –
1912), A POET AND A
SHORT-STORY WRITER,
WAS BORN IN
MANNHEIM, GERMANY.
HIS WRITING HAS BEEN
DESCRIBED AS "A
BOYISH ELABORATION
OF THE MACABRE."
HEYM MADE A FETISH
OF A SCHOOLMATE'S
SUICIDE AND KEPT A
SKULL DECORATED
WITH VINE LEAVES ON
HIS DESK.

THE
AUTOPSY

Georg Heym

Translated by Michael Hamburger

T he dead man lay naked and alone on a white table in the great theater, in the oppressive whiteness, the cruel sobriety of the operating theater that seemed to be vibrating still with the screams of unending torment.

The noon sun covered him and caused the livid spots on his forehead to awaken; it conjured up a bright green out of his naked belly and made it swell like a great sack filled with water.

His body was like the brilliant calyx of a giant flower, a mysterious plant from the Indian jungles which someone had shyly laid down at the altar of death.

Splendid shades of red and blue grew along his loins, and the great wound below his navel, which emitted a terrible odor, split open slowly in the heat like a great red furrow.

The doctors entered. A few kindly men in white coats, with duelling scars and gold pince-nez.

They went up to the dead man and looked at him with interest and professional comments.

They took their dissecting instruments out of white cupboards, white boxes full of hammers, bonesaws with strong teeth, files, horrible batteries of tweezers, little cases full of enormous needles that seemed to cry out incessantly for flesh like the curved beaks of vultures.

They commenced their gruesome work. They were like terrible torturers. The blood flowed over their hands which they plunged ever more deeply into the cold corpse, pulling out its contents, like white cooks drawing a goose.

The intestines coiled around their arms, greenish-yellow snakes, and the excrement dripped on their coats, a warm, putrid fluid. They punctured the bladder. Cold urine glittered inside it like a yellow wine. They poured it into large bowls; it had a sharp and caustic stench like ammonia. But the dead man slept. Patiently he suffered them to tug him this way and that, to pull at his hair. He slept.

And while the blows of the hammer resounded on his head, a dream, the remnant of love in him, awoke like a torch shining into his night.

In front of the large window a great wide sky opened, full of small white clouds that floated in the light, in the afternoon quiet, like small white gods. And the swallows traveled high up in the blue, trembling in the warm July sun.

The dead man's black blood trickled over the blue putrescence of his forehead. It condensed in the heat to a terrible cloud, and the decay of death crept over him with its brightly colored talons. His skin began to flow apart, his belly grew white as an eel's under the greedy fingers of the doctors, who were bathing their arms up to the elbows in his moist flesh.

Decay pulled the dead man's mouth apart. He seemed to smile. He dreamed of a blissful star, of a fragrant summer evening. His dissolving lips quivered as though under a light kiss.

How I love you. I loved you so much. Shall I tell you how much I loved you? When you walked through the poppy fields, yourself a fragrant poppy flame, you had drawn the whole evening into yourself. And your dress that blew about your ankles was like a wave of fire in the glow of the setting sun. But you inclined your head in the light, and your hair still burned and flamed with all my kisses.

So you walked away, looking back at me all the time. And the lamp in your hand swayed like a glowing rose in the dusk long after you had gone.

I shall see you again tomorrow. Here, under the chapel window; here, where the candlelight pours through and changes your hair into a golden forest; here, where the narcissi cling to your ankles, tender as tender kisses.

I shall see you again every night at the hour of dusk. We shall never leave each other. How I love you! Shall I tell you how much I love you?

And the dead man trembled softly with bliss on his white mortuary table, while the iron chisel in the doctor's hand broke open the bones of his temple.

PART FIVE
MIND-BOGGLERS

◆

FRITZ LEIBER IS AN AMERICAN BORN IN 1910. HE WAS AN ACTOR BEFORE HE TOOK UP SCIENCE-FICTION WRITING. HE HAS TWICE WON THE COVETED HUGO AWARD FOR SF WRITING, AND HIS NOVELS INCLUDE *THE BIG TIME* AND *THE WANDERER*.

MARIANA

Fritz Leiber

M ariana had been living in the big villa and hating the tall pine trees around it for what seemed like an eternity when she found the secret panel in the master control panel of the house.

The secret panel was simply a narrow blank of aluminum — she'd thought of it as room for more switches if they ever needed any, perish the thought! — between the air-conditioning controls and the gravity controls. Above the switches for the three-dimensional TV but below those for the robot butler and maids.

Jonathan had told her not to fool with the master control panel while he was in the city, because she would wreck anything electrical, so when the secret panel came loose under her aimlessly questing fingers and fell to the solid rock floor of the patio with a musical *twing* her first reaction was fear.

Then she saw it was only a small blank oblong of sheet aluminum that had fallen and that in the space it had covered was a column of six little switches. Only the top one was identified. Tiny glowing letters beside it spelled TREES and it was on.

When Jonathan got home from the city that evening she gathered her courage and told him about it. He was neither particularly angry nor impressed.

"Of course there's a switch for the trees," he informed her deflatingly, motioning the robot butler to cut his steak. "Didn't you know they were radio trees? I didn't want to wait twenty-five years for them and they couldn't grow in this rock anyway. A station in the city broadcasts a master pine tree and sets like ours pick it up and project it around homes. It's vulgar but convenient."

After a bit she asked timidly, "Jonathan, are the radio pine trees ghostly as you drive through them?"

"Of course not! They're solid as this house and the rock under it—to the eye and to the touch too. A person could even climb them. If you ever stirred outside you'd know these things. The city station transmits pulses of alternating matter at sixty cycles a second. The science of it is over your head."

She ventured one more question: "Why did they have the tree switch covered up?"

"So you wouldn't monkey with it—same as the fine controls on the TV. And so you wouldn't get ideas and start changing the trees. It would unsettle *me*, let me tell you, to come home to oaks one day and birches the next. I like consistency and I like pines." He looked at them out of the dining-room picture window and grunted with satisfaction.

She had been meaning to tell him about hating the pines, but that discouraged her and she dropped the topic.

About noon the next day, however, she went to the secret panel and switched off the pine trees and quickly turned around to watch them.

At first nothing happened and she was beginning to think that Jonathan was wrong again, as he so often was though would never admit, but then they began to waver and specks of pale green light churned across them and then they faded and were gone, leaving behind only an intolerably bright single point of light—just as when the TV is switched off. The star hovered motionless for what seemed a long time, then backed away and raced off toward the horizon.

Now that the pine trees were out of the way Mariana could see the real landscape. It was flat gray rock, endless miles of it, exactly the same as the rock on which the house was set and which formed the floor of the patio. It was the same in every direciton. One black two-lane road drove straight across it—nothing more.

She disliked the view almost at once—it was dreadfully lonely and depressing. She switched the gravity to moon-normal and danced about dreamily, floating over the middle-of-the-room bookshelves and the grand piano and even having the robot maids dance with her, but it did not cheer her. About two o'clock she went to switch on the pine trees again, as she had intended to do in any case before Jonathan came home and was furious.

However, she found there had been changes in the column of six little switches. The TREES switch no longer had its glowing name. She remembered that it had been the top one, but the top one would not turn on again. She tried to force it from "off" to "on" but it would not move.

All of the rest of the afternoon she sat on the steps outside the front door watching the black two-lane road. Never a car or a person came into view until Jonathan's tan roadster appeared, seeming at first to hang motionless in the distance and then to move only like a microscopic snail although she knew he always drove at top speed—it was one of the reasons she would never get in the car with him.

Jonathan was not as furious as she had feared. "Your own damn fault for meddling with it," he said curtly. "Now we'll have to get a man out here. Dammit, I hate to eat supper looking at nothing but those rocks! Bad enough driving through them twice a day."

She asked him haltingly about the barrenness of the landscape and the absence of neighbors.

"Well, you wanted to live *way out*," he told her. "You wouldn't ever have known about it if you hadn't turned off the trees."

"There's one other thing I've got to bother you with, Jonathan," she said. "Now the second switch — the one next below — has got a name that glows. It just says HOUSE. It's turned on — I haven't touched it! Do you suppose . . ."

"I want to look at this," he said, bounding up from the couch and slamming his martini-on-the-rocks tumbler down on the tray of the robot maid so that she rattled. "I bought this house as solid, but there are swindles. Ordinarily I'd spot a broadcast style in a flash, but they just might have slipped me a job relayed from some other planet or solar system. Fine thing if me and fifty other multi-megabuck men were spotted around in identical houses, each thinking his was unique."

"But if the house is based on rock like it is . . ."

"That would just make it easier for them to pull the trick, you dumb bunny!"

They reached the master control panel. "There it is," she said helpfully, jabbing out a finger . . . and hit the HOUSE switch.

For a moment nothing happened, then a white churning ran across the ceiling, the walls and furniture started to swell and bubble like cold lava, and then they were alone on a rock table big as three tennis courts. Even the master control panel was gone. The only thing that was left was a slender rod coming out of the gray stone at their feet and bearing at the top, like some mechanistic fruit, a small block with the six switches — that and an intolerably bright star hanging in the air where the master bedroom had been.

Mariana pushed frantically at the HOUSE switch, but it was unlabeled now and locked in the "off" position, although she threw her weight at it stiff-armed.

The upstairs star sped off like an incendiary bullet, but its last flashbulb glare showed her Jonathan's face set in lines of fury. He lifted his hands like talons.

"You little idiot!" he screamed, coming at her.

"No, Jonathan, no!" she wailed, backing off, but he kept coming.

She realized that the block of switches had broken off in her hands. The third switch had a glowing name now: JONATHAN. She flipped it.

As his fingers dug into her bare shoulders they seemed to turn to foam rubber, then to air. His face and gray flannel suit seethed iridescently, like a leprous ghost's, then melted and ran. His star, smaller than that of the house but much closer, seared her eyes. When she opened them again there was nothing at all left of the star or Jonathan but a dancing dark after-image like a black tennis ball.

She was alone on an infinite flat rock plain under the cloudless, star-specked sky.

The fourth switch had its glowing name now: STARS.

It was almost dawn by her radium-dialed wristwatch and she was thoroughly chilled, when she finally decided to switch off the stars. She did not want to do it — in their slow wheeling across the sky they were the last sign of orderly reality — but it seemed the only move she could make.

She wondered what the fifth switch would say. ROCKS? AIR? Or even . . . ?

She switched off the stars.

The Milky Way, arching in all its unalterable glory, began to churn, its component stars darting about like midges. Soon only one remained, brighter even than Sirius or Venus — until it jerked back, fading, and darted to infinity.

The fifth switch said DOCTOR and it was not on but off.

An inexplicable terror welled up in Mariana. She did not even want to touch

161

the fifth switch. She set the block of switches down on the rock and backed away from it.

But she dared not go far in the starless dark. She huddled down and waited for dawn. From time to time she looked at her watch dial and at the night-light glow of the switch-label a dozen yards away.

It seemed to be growing much colder.

She read her watch dial. It was two hours past sunrise. She remembered they had taught her in third grade that the sun was just one more star.

She went back and sat down beside the block of switches and picked it up with a shudder and flipped the fifth switch.

The rock grew soft and crisply fragrant under her and lapped up over her legs and then slowly turned white.

She was sitting in a hospital bed in a small blue room with a white pin-stripe.

A sweet, mechanical voice came out of the wall, saying, "You have interrupted the wish-fulfillment therapy by your own decision. If you now recognize your sick depression and are willing to accept help, the doctor will come to you. If not, you are at liberty to return to the wish-fulfillment therapy and pursue it to its ultimate conclusion."

Mariana looked down. She still had the block of switches in her hands and the fifth switch still read DOCTOR.

The wall said, "I assume from your silence that you will accept treatment. The doctor will be with you immediately."

The inexplicable terror returned to Mariana with compulsive intensity.

She switched off the doctor.

She was back in the starless dark. The rocks had grown very much colder. She could feel icy feathers falling on her face — snow.

She lifted the block of switches and saw, to her unutterable relief, that the sixth and last switch now read, in tiny glowing letters: MARIANA.

FRED HOYLE IS A
BRITISH PROFESSOR
WHO WRITES NOVELS
AND SHORT STORIES
AND LOVES TO DABBLE
IN MATHEMATICS AND
ASTRONOMY.

BLACKMAIL

Fred Hoyle

A ngus Carruthers was a wayward, impish genius. Genius is not the same thing as high ability. Men of great talent commonly spread their efforts, often very effectively, over a wide front. The true genius devotes the whole of his skill, his energies, his intelligence, to a particular objective, which he pursues unrelentingly.

Early in life, Carruthers became skeptical of human superiority over other animals. Already in his early teens he understood exactly where the difference lies — it lies in the ability of humans to pool their knowledge through speech, in the ability through speech to educate the young. The challenging problem to his keen mind was to find a system of communication, every bit as powerful as language, that could be made available to others of the higher animals. The basic idea was not original; it was the determination to carry the idea through to its conclusion that was new. Carruthers pursued his objective inflexibly down the years.

Gussie had no patience with people who talked and chattered to animals. If animals had the capacity to understand language wouldn't they have done it already, he said, thousands of years ago? Talk was utterly and completely pointless. You were just damned stupid if you thought you were going to teach English to your pet dog or cat. The thing to do was to understand the world from the point of view of the dog or cat. Once you'd got yourself into *their* system it would be time enough to think about trying to get them into *your* system.

Gussie had no close friends. I suppose I was about as near to being a friend as anyone, yet even I would see him only perhaps once in six months. There was always something refreshingly different when you happened to run into him. He might have grown a black spade beard, or he might just have had a crew-cut. He might be wearing a flowing cape, or he might be neatly tailored in a Bond Street suit. He always trusted me well enough to show off his latest experiments. At the least they were remarkable, at the best they went far beyond anything I had heard of, or read about. To my repeated suggestions that he simply must "publish" he always responded with a long wheezy laugh. To me it seemed just plain common sense to publish, if only to raise money for the experiments, but Gussie obviously didn't see it this way. How he managed for money, I could never discover. I supposed him to have a private income, which was very likely correct.

One day I received a note asking me to proceed to such-and-such an address, sometime near 4 P.M. on a certain Saturday. There was nothing unusual in my receiving a note, for Carruthers had got in touch with me several times before in this way. It was the address which came as the surprise, a house in a Croydon suburb. On previous occasions I had always gone out to some decrepit barn of a place in remotest Hertfordshire. The idea of Gussie in Croydon somehow didn't fit. I was sufficiently intrigued to put off a previous appointment and to hie myself along at the appropriate hour.

My wild notion that Carruthers might have got himself well and truly wed, that he might have settled down in a nine-to-five job, turned out to be quite wrong. The big tortoiseshell spectacles he had sported at our previous meeting were gone, replaced by plain steel rims. His lank black hair was medium long this time. He had a lugubrious look about him, as if he had just been rehearsing the part of Quince in *A Midsummer Night's Dream*.

"Come in," he wheezed.

"What's the idea, living in these parts?" I asked as I slipped off my overcoat. For answer, he broke into a whistling, croaking laugh.

"Better take a look, in there."

The door to which Gussie pointed was closed. I was pretty sure I would find animals "in there," and so it proved. Although the room was darkened by a drawn curtain, there was sufficient light for me to see three creatures crouched around a television set. They were intently watching the second half of a game of Rugby League football. There was a cat with a big rust-red patch on the top of its head. There was a poodle, which cocked an eye at me for a fleeting second as I went in, and there was a furry animal sprawled in a big armchair. As I went in, I had the odd impression of the animal lifting a paw, as if by way of greeting. Then I realized it was a small brown bear.

I had known Gussie long enough now, I had seen enough of his work, to realize that any comment in words would be ridiculous and superfluous. I had long ago learned the right procedure, to do exactly the same thing as the animals themselves were doing. Since I have always been partial to rugby, I was able to settle down quite naturally to watch the game in company with this amazing trio. Every so often I found myself catching the bright, alert eyes of the bear. I soon realized that, whereas I was mainly interested in the run of the ball, the animals were mainly interested in the tackling, *qua* tackling. Once when a player was brought down particularly heavily there was a muffled yap from the poodle, instantly answered by a grunt from the bear.

After perhaps twenty minutes I was startled by a really loud bark from the dog, there being nothing at all in the game to warrant such an outburst. Evidently the dog wanted to attract the attention of the engrossed bear, for when the bear looked up quizzically the dog pointed a dramatic paw toward a clock standing a couple of yards to the left of the television set. Immediately the bear lumbered from its chair to the set. It fumbled with the controls. There was a click, and to my astonishment we were on another channel. A wrestling bout had just begun.

The bear rolled back to its chair. It stretched itself, resting lazily on the base of the spine, arms raised with the claws cupped behind the head. One of the wrestlers spun the other violently. There was a loud thwack as the unfortunate fellow cracked his head on a ring post. At this, the cat let out the strangest animal noise I had ever heard. Then it settled down into a deep powerful purr.

I had seen and heard enough. As I quitted the room the bear waved me out, much in the style of royalty and visiting heads of state. I found Gussie placidly drinking tea in what was evidently the main sitting room of the house. To my frenzied requests to be told exactly what it meant, Gussie responded with his usual asthmatic laugh. Instead of answering my questions he asked some of his own.

"I want your advice, professionally as a lawyer. There's nothing illegal in the animals watching television, is there? Or in the bear switching the programs?"

"How could there be?"

"The situation's a bit complicated. Here, take a look at this."

Carruthers handed me a typewritten list. It covered a week of television programs. If this represented viewing by the animals the set must have been switched on more or less continuously. The programs were all of a type, sport, Westerns, suspense plays, films of violence.

"What they love," said Gussie by way of explanation, "is the sight of humans bashing themselves to pieces. Really, of course, it's more or less the usual popular taste, only a bit more so."

I noticed the name of a well-known rating firm on the letterhead.

"What's this heading here? I mean, what's all this to do with the TV ratings?"

Gussie fizzed and crackled like a soda-siphon.

"That's exactly the point. This house here is one of the odd few hundreds used in compiling the weekly ratings. That's why I asked if there was anything wrong in Bingo doing the switching."

"You don't mean viewing by those animals is going into the ratings?"

"Not only here, but in three other houses I've bought. I've got a team of chaps in each of them. Bears take quite naturally to the switching business."

"There'll be merry hell to pay if it comes out. Can't you see what the papers will make of it?"

"Very clearly indeed."

The point hit me at last. Gussie could hardly have come on four houses by chance, all of which just happened to be hooked up to the TV rating system. As far as I could see there wasn't anything illegal in what he'd done, so long as he didn't make any threats or demands. As if he read my thoughts, he pushed a slip of paper under my nose. It was a check for £50,000.

"Unsolicited," he wheezed, "came out of the blue. From somebody in the advertising game, I suppose. Hush money. The problem is, do I put myself in the wrong if I cash it?"

Before I could form an opinion on this tricky question there came a tinkling of breaking glass.

"Another one gone," Gussie muttered. "I haven't been able to teach Bingo to use the vertical or horizontal holds. Whenever anything goes wrong, or the program goes off for a minute, he hammers away at the thing. It's always the tube that goes."

"It must be quite a costly business."

"Averages about a dozen a week. I always keep a spare set ready. Be a good fellow and give me a hand with it. They'll get pretty testy if we don't move smartly."

We lifted what seemed like a brand-new set from out of a cupboard. Each gripping an end of it, we edged our way to the television snuggery. From inside, I was now aware of a strident uproar, compounded from the bark of a dog, the grunt of a bear, and the shrill moan of a red-headed cat. It was the uproar of animals suddenly denied their intellectual pabulum.

DAMON KNIGHT (1922–)
IS A NOTED WRITER AND
EDITOR OF SCIENCE
FICTION. HIS WORKS
DEAL WITH THE
PROBLEMS OF
MIND-CONTROLLED
SOCIETIES, CLONING,
AND ALIEN INVASIONS.
HIS BETTER KNOWN
NOVELS INCLUDE *THE
SUN SABOTEURS* AND
MIND SWITCH.

THE HANDLER

Damon Knight

When the big man came in, there was a movement in the
room like a lot of bird dogs pointing. Piano player quits
pounding, the two singing drunks shut up, all the beautiful people with cocktails in their hands stop talking and laughing.

"Pete!" the nearest women shrilled, and he walked straight into
the room, arms around two girls, hugging them tight. "How's my
sweetheart? Susy, you look good enough to eat, but I had it for
lunch. George, you pirate"—he let go both girls, grabbed a bald
blushing little man and thumped him on the arm—"you were great, sweetheart,
I mean it, really great. Now HEAR THIS!" he shouted, over all the voices that
were clamoring Pete this, Pete that.

Somebody put a martini in his hand and he stood holding it, bronzed and tall in
his dinner jacket, teeth gleaming white as his shirt cuffs. "We had a show!" he
told them.

A shriek of agreement went up, a babble of did we have a *show* my God Pete
listen a *show* —

He held up his hand. "It was a good show!"

Another shriek and babble.

"The sponsor kinda liked it—he just signed for another one in the fall!"

A shriek, a roar, people clapping, jumping up and down. The big man tried to
say something else, but gave up, grinning, while men and women crowded up to
him. They were all trying to shake his hand, talk in his ear, put their arms
around him.

"I love ya *all*!" he shouted. "Now what do you say, let's live a little!"

The murmuring started again as people sorted themselves out. There was a

---

clinking from the bar. "Jesus, Pete," a skinny pop-eyed little guy was saying, crouching in adoration, "when you dropped that fishbowl I thought I'd pee myself, honest to God—"

The big man let out a bark of happy laughter. "Yeah, I can still see the look on your face. And the fish, flopping all over the stage. So what can I *do*, I get down there on my knees—" The big man did so, bending over and staring at imaginary fish on the floor. "And I say, 'Well, fellows, back to the drawing board!'"

Screams of laughter as the big man stood up. The party was arranging itself around him in arcs of concentric circles, with people in the back standing on sofas and the piano bench so they could see. Somebody yelled, "Sing the goldfish song, Pete!"

Shouts of approval, please-do-Pete, the goldfish song.

"Okay, okay." Grinning, the big man sat on the arm of a chair and raised his glass. "And a vun, and a doo—vere's de moosic?" A scuffle at the piano bench. Somebody banged out a few chords. The big man made a comic face and sang, "Ohhh...how I wish...I was a little fish...and when I want some quail...I'd flap my little tail."

Laughter, the girls laughing louder than anybody and their red mouths farther open. One flushed blonde had her hand on the big man's knee, and another was sitting close behind him.

"But seriously—" the big man shouted. More laughter.

"No, seriously," he said in a vibrant voice as the room quieted, "I want to tell you in all seriousness I couldn't have done it alone. And incidentally I see we have some foreigners, litvaks and other members of the press here tonight, so I want to introduce all the important people. First of all, George here, the three-fingered band leader—and there isn't a guy in the world could have done what he did this afternoon—George, I love ya." He hugged the blushing little bald man.

"Next my real sweetheart, Ruthie, where are ya. Honey, you were the greatest, really perfect—I mean it, baby—" He kissed a dark girl in a red dress who cried a little and hid her face on his broad shoulder. "And Frank—" He reached down and grabbed the skinny pop-eyed guy by the sleeve. "What can I tell you? A sweetheart?" The skinny guy was blinking, all choked up; the big man thumped him on the back. "Sol and Ernie and Mack, my writers, Shakespeare should have been so lucky—" One by one, they came up to shake the big man's hand as he called their names; the women kissed him and cried. "My stand-in," the big man was calling out, and "my caddy," and "now," he said, as the room quieted a little, people flushed and sore-throated with enthusiasm, "I want you to meet my handler."

The room fell silent. The big man looked thoughtful and startled, as if he had had a sudden pain. Then he stopped moving. He sat without breathing or blinking his eyes. After a moment there was a jerky motion behind him. The girl who was sitting on the arm of the chair got up and moved away. The big man's dinner jacket split open in the back, and a little man climbed out. He had a perspiring brown face under a shock of black hair. He was a very small man, almost a dwarf, stoop-shouldered and round-backed in a sweaty brown singlet and shorts. He climbed out of the cavity in the big man's body, and closed the dinner jacket carefully. The big man sat motionless and his face was doughy.

The little man got down, wetting his lips nervously. Hello, Fred, a few people said. "Hello," Fred called, waving his hand. He was about forty, with a big nose and big soft brown eyes. His voice was cracked and uncertain. "Well, we sure put on a show, didn't we?"

Sure did, Fred, they said politely. He wiped his brow with the back of his hand. "Hot in there," he explained, with an apologetic grin. Yes, I guess it must be Fred, they said. People around the outskirts of the crowd were beginning to turn away, form conversational groups; the hum of talk rose higher. "Say, Tim, I wonder if I could have something to drink," the little man said. "I don't like to leave him — you know — " He gestured toward the silent big man.

"Sure, Fred, what'll it be?"

"Oh — you know — a glass of beer?"

Tim brought him a beer in a pilsener glass and he drank it thirstily, his brown eyes darting nervously from side to side. A lot of people were sitting down now; one or two were at the door leaving.

"Well," the little man said to a passing girl, "Ruthie, that was quite a moment there, when the fishbowl busted, wasn't it?"

"Huh? Excuse me, honey. I didn't hear you." She bent nearer.

"Oh — well, it don't matter. Nothing."

She patted him on the shoulder once, and took her hand away. "Well, excuse me, sweetie, I have to catch Robbins before he leaves." She went on toward the door.

The little man put his beer glass down and sat, twisting his knobby hands together. The bald man and the pop-eyed man were the only ones still sitting near him. An anxious smile flickered on his lips; he glanced at one face, then another. "Well," he began, "that's one show under our belts, huh, fellows, but I guess we got to start, you know, thinking about — "

"Listen, Fred," said the bald man seriously, leaning forward to touch him on the wrist, "why don't you get back inside?"

The little man looked at him for a moment with sad hound-dog eyes, then ducked his head, embarrassed. He stood up uncertainly, swallowed and said, "Well — " He climbed up on the chair behind the big man, opened the back of the dinner jacket and put his legs in one at a time. A few people were watching him, unsmiling. "Thought I'd take it easy a while," he said weakly, "but I guess — " He reached in and gripped something with both hands, then swung himself inside. His brown, uncertain face disappeared.

The big man blinked suddenly and stood up. "Well, *hey* there," he called, "what's a matter with this party anyway? Let's see some life, some action — " Faces were lighting up around him. People began to move in closer. "What I mean, let me hear that beat!"

The big man began clapping his hands rhythmically. The piano took it up. Other people began to clap. "What I mean, are we alive or just waiting for the wagon to pick us up? How's that again, can't *hear* you!" A roar of pleasure as he cupped his hand to his ear. "Well, come on, let me hear it!" A louder roar. Pete, Pete; a gabble of voices. "I got nothing against Fred," said the bald man earnestly in the middle of the noise. "I mean for a square he's a nice guy." "Know what you mean," said the pop-eyed man, "I mean like he doesn't *mean* it." "Sure," said the bald man, "but, Jesus, that sweaty undershirt and all . . . " Then they both burst out laughing as the big man made a comic face, tongue lolling, eyes crossed. Pete, Pete, Pete; the room was really jumping; it was a great party, and everything was all right far into the night.

ENRIQUE ANDERSON
IMBERT WAS BORN IN
ARGENTINA ON
FEBRUARY 12, 1910. HE
HAS BEEN AN AMERICAN
CITIZEN SINCE 1952.
IMBERT'S FICTION IS
CHARACTERIZED BY
MAGIC REALISM. THIS
MEANS THAT A STORY
BEGINS WITH A
REALISTIC SITUATION
THAT IS DEVELOPED
LOGICALLY TO A
FANTASTIC
CONCLUSION.

THE CRIME
IN THE
ATTIC

Enrique Anderson Imbert

Translated by Isabel Reade

Detective Hackett knocked anxiously at the door of Sir Eugene's mansion. Perhaps he was too late! Perhaps they had already killed him!

When at last the servant opened the door, Hackett rushed in, shouting. There came running from different directions an old lady — Lady Malver, evidently — a young man with bulging eyes, and a gentleman who seemed to be always smiling.

"Where is Sir Eugene? Quickly, quickly! It's a matter of life and death!"

"In the attic, developing his photographs," the servant managed to say.

And they all dashed up the stairs: the men, jumping the steps two at a time; Lady Malver, slowly, like a caterpillar.

The attic door was locked. They knocked.

"Sir Eugene, Sir Eugene! Are you there?"

From the other side they heard a voice, tremulous, anguished:

"Ah, come, please!"

Hackett struggled with the doorknob, but the bolt was drawn.

"Unlock the door, Sir Eugene!"

Lady Malver was there by this time, out of breath:

"Eugene," she gasped.

They heard, from the inside, the turning of the lock, then something like panting, the sound of a body collapsing. . . . And a silence.

Hackett pushed the door again. Now it gave way. They all went in tumultuously.

At first they could see nothing. Only, at one side, the cloudy eye of the red lamp. The darkness was round, dense, reddish, pulpy. And then they discovered in the center (it looked like the core of a fruit!) Sir Eugene, hard, lying full length. Someone turned on a white light. A dagger was sprouting from Sir Eugene's back, like a tiny wing.

Hackett inspected the room. There were no exits. It was a hermetic world, like a peach with the corpse inside, in the middle. He tapped the floor, the walls; he studied the position of the dead man, of the weapon. . . .

After a while he went to the door, locked it, put the key in his pocket and drew his revolver.

"The murderer," he said, looking at everybody one by one, "is here. The murderer took advantage of the charge in the darkness to stab Sir Eugene."

There were protests.

Hackett answered them all, discarding impossibilities. The death was recent. Murder and not suicide. There was no means of escape even for a monkey. Nor could the dagger have been thrown at him from a distance. The room had no mechanisms.

The old lady, her face livid, proposed timidly:

"What if it were something supernatural? I don't know. . . those horrible negatives, there under the red light. . . . They look as though they were made of flesh, soft and pale like a degenerate's. . . . Perhaps, when the white light went on, those negatives took away the secret. . . . Perhaps they took away the criminal himself. . . . I mean. . . . Some supernatural murderer."

"Supernatural?" the detective commented sarcastically. "There is nothing supernatural."

Then, hearing that "There is nothing supernatural!" all of them, Lady Malver herself and even the corpse, burst out laughing like a fountain with many jets. A great laughter in a chorus, simultaneous, a single laugh laughed by the six mouths in a single shaking of concerted rhythms. And, without stopping laughing, the figures of Hackett, Sir Eugene, Lady Malver, the servant, the young man with bulging eyes, and the gentleman with the smiling mouth began shrivelling, began fading away like six pale flames. Then the individuals came together, through the air, with the determination of will-o'-the-wisps, and blended into a single transparency; and from within that mass was remade the original form of the goblin. He was the goblin of the house, the goblin addicted to detective stories.

Puckish, invisible, aerial, licentious, fraudulent, free, the goblin passed through the wall of the locked attic, descended the stairs of the solitary house and went to look in the bookcase for another detective story. How they amused him, those fateful games without chance that men wrote! Especially, it amused him to play all the roles.

176

SLAWOMIR MROZEK
(1930–) WAS BORN IN
POLAND. A SATIRIC
DRAMATIST AND
SHORT-FICTION
WRITER, HE ATTACKS
GOVERNMENT AND
BUREAUCRATIC
STUPIDITY IN HIS
WORKS. *THE POLICE*
AND *TANGO* ARE TWO
OF HIS PLAYS.

178

THE ELEPHANT

Slawomir Mrozek

Translated by Konrad Syrop

T he director of the Zoological Gardens has shown himself to be an upstart. He regarded his animals simply as stepping stones on the road of his own career. He was indifferent to the educational importance of his establishment. In his Zoo the giraffe had a short neck, the badger had no burrow and the whistlers, having lost all interest, whistled rarely and with some reluctance. These short-comings should not have been allowed, especially as the Zoo was often visited by parties of schoolchildren.

The Zoo was in a provincial town, and it was short of some of the most important animals, among them the elephant. Three thousand rabbits were a poor substitute for the noble giant. However, as our country developed, the gaps were being filled in a well-planned manner. On the occasion of the anniversary of the liberation, on 22nd July, the Zoo was notified that it had at long last been allocated an elephant. All the staff, who were devoted to their work, rejoiced at this news. All the greater was their surprise when they learnt that the director had sent a letter to Warsaw, renouncing the allocation and putting forward a plan for obtaining an elephant by more economic means.

"I, and all the staff," he had written, "are fully aware how heavy a burden falls upon the shoulders of Polish miners and foundry men because of the elephant. Desirous of reducing our costs, I suggest that the elephant mentioned in your communication should be replaced by one of our own procurement. We can make an elephant out of rubber, of the correct size, fill it with air and place it behind railings. It will be carefully painted the correct colour and even on close inspection will be indistinguishable from the real animal. It is well known that the elephant is a sluggish animal and it does not run and jump about. In the

179

notice on the railings we can state that this particular elephant is exceptionally sluggish. The money saved in this way can be turned to the purchase of a jet plane or the conservation of some church monument.

"Kindly note that both the idea and its execution are my modest contribution to the common task and struggle.

"I am, etc."

This communication must have reached a soulless official, who regarded his duties in a purely bureaucratic manner and did not examine the heart of the matter but, following only the director about reduction of expenditure, accepted the director's plan. On hearing the Ministry's approval, the director issued instructions for the making of the rubber elephant.

The carcass was to have been filled with air by two keepers blowing into it from opposite ends. To keep the operation secret the work was to be completed during the night because the people of the town, having heard that an elephant was joining the Zoo, were anxious to see it. The director insisted on haste also because he expected a bonus, should his idea turn out to be a success.

The two keepers locked themselves in a shed normally housing a workshop, and began to blow. After two hours of hard blowing they discovered that the rubber skin had risen only a few inches above the floor and its bulge in no way resembled an elephant. The night progressed. Outside, human voices were stilled and only the cry of the jackass interrupted the silence. Exhausted, the keepers stopped blowing and made sure that the air already inside the elephant should not escape. They were not young and were unaccustomed to this kind of work.

"If we go on at this rate," said one of them, "we shan't finish before the morning. And what am I to tell my Missus? She'll never believe me if I say that I spent the night blowing up an elephant."

"Quite right," agreed the second keeper. "Blowing up an elephant is not an everyday job. And it's all because our director is a leftist."

They resumed their blowing, but after another half-an-hour they felt too tired to continue. The bulge on the floor was larger but still nothing like the shape of an elephant.

"It's getting harder all the time," said the first keeper.

"It's an uphill job, all right," agreed the second. "Let's have a little rest."

While they were resting, one of them noticed a gas pipe ending in a valve. Could they not fill the elephant with gas? He suggested it to his mate.

They decided to try. They connected the elephant to the gas pipe, turned the valve, and to their joy in a few minutes there was a full-sized beast standing in the shed. It looked real: the enormous body, legs like columns, huge ears and the inevitable trunk. Driven by ambition the director had made sure of having in his Zoo a very large elephant indeed.

"First class," declared the keeper who had the idea of using gas. "Now we can go home."

In the morning the elephant was moved to a special run in a central position, next to the monkey cage. Placed in front of a large real rock it looked fierce and magnificient. A big notice proclaimed: "Particularly sluggish. Hardly moves."

Among the first visitors that morning was a party of children from the local school. The teacher in charge of them was planning to give them an object-lesson about the elephant. He halted the group in front of the animal and began:

"The elephant is a herbivorous mammal. By means of its trunk it pulls out young trees and eats their leaves."

The children were looking at the elephant with enraptured admiration. They were waiting for it to pull out a young tree, but the beast stood still behind its railings.

"... The elephant is a direct descendant of the now extinct mammoth. It's not surprising, therefore, that it's the largest living land animal."

The more conscientious pupils were making notes.

"... Only the whale is heavier than the elephant, but then the whale lives in the sea. We can safely say that on land the elephant reigns supreme."

A slight breeze moved the branches of the trees in the Zoo.

"... The weight of a fully grown elephant is between nine and thirteen thousand pounds."

At that moment the elephant shuddered and rose in the air. For a few seconds it swayed just above the ground but a gust of wind blew it upwards until its mighty silhouette was against the sky. For a short while people on the ground could still see the four circles of its feet, its bulging belly and the trunk, but soon, propelled by the wind, the elephant sailed above the fence and disappeared above the tree-tops. Astonished monkeys in the cage continued staring into the sky.

They found the elephant in the neighboring botanical gardens. It had landed on a cactus and punctured its rubber hide.

The schoolchildren who had witnessed the scene in the Zoo soon started neglecting their studies and turned into hooligans. It is reported that they drink liquor and break windows. And they no longer believe in elephants.

REGINALD C. BRETNOR
WAS BORN IN SIBERIA
BUT HAS LIVED MOST
OF HIS LIFE IN THE
UNITED STATES. HIS
STORIES HAVE
APPEARED IN *GALAXY*
AND *THE MAGAZINE OF
FANTASY AND SCIENCE
FICTION*.

BUG-GETTER

Reginald C. Bretnor

Ambrosius Goshawk was a starving artist. He couldn't afford to starve decently in a garret in Montmartre or Greenwich Village. He lived in a cold, smoke-stained flat in downtown Pittsburgh, a flat furnished with enormously hairy overstuffed objects which always seemed moist, and filled with unsalable paintings. The paintings were all in a style strongly reminiscent of Rembrandt, but with far more than his technical competence. They were absurdly representational.

Goshawk's wife had abandoned him, moving in with a dealer who merchandised thousands of Klee and Mondrian reproductions at $1.98 each. Her note had been scrawled on the back of a nasty demand from his dentist's collection agency. Two shoddy subpoenas lay on the floor next to his landlord's eviction notice. In this litter, unshaven and haggard, sat Ambrosius Goshawk. His left hand held a newspaper clipping, a disquisition on his work by one J. Herman Lort, the nation's foremost authority on Art. His right hand held a palette-knife with which he was desperately scraping little green crickets from the unfinished painting on his easel, a nude for which Mrs. Goshawk has posed.

The apartment was full of little green crickets. So, for that matter, was the Eastern half of the country. But Ambrosius Goshawk was not concerned with them as a plague. They were simply an intensely personal, utterly shattering Last Straw—and, as he scraped, he was thinking the strongest thoughts he had ever thought.

He had been thinking them for some hours, and they had, of course, traveled far out into the inhabited Universe. That was why, at three minutes past two in the afternoon, there was a whirr at the window, a click as it was pushed open

---

183

from the outside, and a thud as a small bucket-shaped spaceship landed on the unpaid-for carpet. A hatch opened, and a gnarled, undersized being stepped out.

"Well," he said, with what might have been a slightly curdled Bulgarian accent, "here I am."

Ambrosius Goshawk flipped a cricket over his shoulder, glared, and said decisively, "No, I will *not* take you to my leader." Then he started working on another cricket who had his feet stuck on a particularly intimate part of Mrs. Goshawk's anatomy.

"I am not interested with your leader," replied the being, unstrapping something that looked like a super-gadgety spray-gun. "You have thought for me, because you are wanting an extermination. I am the Exterminator. Johnny-with-the-spot, that is me. Pronounce me your troubles."

Ambrosius Goshawk put down his palette-knife. "What won't I think of next?" he exclaimed. "Little man, because of the manner of your arrival, your alleged business, and my state of mind, I will take you quite seriously. Seat yourself."

Then, starting with his failure to get a scholarship back in art school he worked down through his landlord, his dentist, his wife, to the clipping by J. Herman Lort, from which he read at some length, coming finally to the following passage:

"...and it is in the work of these pseudo-creative people, of self-styled 'artists' like Ambrosius Goshawk, whose clumsily crafted imitations of photography must be a thorn in the flesh of every truly sensitive and creative critical mind, that the perceptive collector will realize the deeply-researched validness of the doctrine I have explained in my book *The Creative Critical Intellect* — that true Art can be 'created' only by such an intellect when adequately trained in an appropriately staffed institution, 'created' needless to say out of the vast treasury of natural and accidental-type forms — out of driftwood and bird-droppings, out of torn-up roots and cracked rocks — and that all the rest is a snare and a delusion, nay! an outright fraud."

Ambrosius Goshawk threw the clipping down. "You'd think," he cried out, "that mortal man could stand no more. And now —" he pointed at the invading insects — "*now there's this!*"

"So," asked the being, "what is this?"

Ambrosius Goshawk took a deep breath, counted to seven, and screamed, "*CRICKETS!*" hysterically.

"It is simple," said the being. "I will exterminate. My fee —"

"Fee?" Goshawk interrupted him bitterly. "How can *I* pay a fee?"

"My fee will be paintings. Six you will give. In advance. Then I exterminate. After, it is one dozen more."

Goshawk decided that other worlds must have wealthy eccentrics, but he made no demur. He watched while the Exterminator put six paintings aboard, and he waved a dizzy goodbye as the spaceship took off. Then he went back to prying the crickets of Mrs. Goshawk.

The Exterminator returned two years later. However, his spaceship did not have to come in through the window. It simply sailed down past the towers of Ambrosius Goshawk's Florida castle into a fountained courtyard patterned after somewhat simpler ones in the Taj Mahal, and landed among a score of young women whose figures and costumes suggested a handsomely modernized Mussulman heaven. Some were splashing raw in the fountains. Some were lounging around Goshawk's easel, hoping he might try to seduce them. Two

184

were standing by with swatters, alert for the little green crickets which occasionally happened along.

The Exterminator did not notice Goshawk's curt nod. "How hard to have find you," he chuckled, "ha-ha! Half-miles from north, I see some big palaces, ha, so! all marbles. From the south, even bigger, one Japanese castles. Who has built?"

Goshawk rudely replied that the palaces belonged to several composers, sculptors, and writers, that the Japanese castle was the whim of an elderly poetess, and that the Exterminator would have to excuse him because he was busy.

The Exterminator paid no attention. "See how has changing, your world," he exclaimed, rubbing his hands. "All artists have many success. With yachts, with Rolls-Royces, with minks, diamonds, many round ladies. Now I take twelve more paintings."

"Beat it," snarled Goshawk. "You'll get no more paintings from me!"

The Exterminator was taken aback. "You are having not happy?" he asked. "You have not liking all this? I have done job like my promise. You must paying one dozen more picture."

A cricket hopped onto the nude on which Goshawk was working. He threw his brush to the ground. "I'll pay you nothing!" he shouted. "Why, you fake, you did nothing at all! *Any* good artist can succeed nowadays, but it's no thanks to *you! Look at 'em* — there are as many of these damned crickets as ever!"

The Exterminator's jaw dropped in astonishment. For a moment, he goggled at Goshawk.

Then, *"Crickets?"* he croaked. "My God! *I* have thought you said *critics!*"

JULIO CORTAZÁR (1914-)
WAS BORN IN
ARGENTINA BUT NOW
LIVES IN FRANCE.
CORTAZÁR'S FICTION, IN
ITS USE OF FANTASTIC
SETTINGS AND PLOTS,
RESEMBLES THAT OF
JORGE LUIS BORGES,
ANOTHER SOUTH
AMERICAN WRITER.

CONTINUITY OF PARKS

Julio Cortazár

Translated by Paul Blackburn

He had begun to read the novel a few days before. He had put it down because of some urgent business conferences, opened it again on his way back to the estate by train; he permitted himself a slowly growing interest in the plot, in the characterizations. That afternoon, after writing a letter giving his power of attorney and discussing a matter of joint ownership with the manager of his estate, he returned to the book in the tranquillity of his study which looked out upon the park with its oaks. Sprawled in his favorite armchair, its back toward the door — even the possibility of an intrusion would have irritated him, had he thought of it — he let his left hand caress repeatedly the green velvet upholstery and set to reading the final chapters. He remembered effortlessly the names and his mental image of the characters; the novel spread its glamour over him almost at once. He tasted the almost perverse pleasure of disengaging himself line by line from the things around him, and at the same time feeling his head rest comfortably on the green velvet of the chair with its high back, sensing that the cigarettes rested within reach of his hand, that beyond the great windows the air of afternoon danced under the oak trees in the park. Word by word, licked up by the sordid dilemma of the hero and heroine, letting himself be absorbed to the point where the images settled down and took on color and movement, he was witness to the final encounter in the mountain cabin. The woman arrived first, apprehensive; now the lover came in, his face cut by the backlash of a branch. Admirably, she stanched the blood with her kisses, but he rebuffed her caresses, he had not come to perform again the ceremonies of a secret passion, protected by a world of dry leaves and furtive paths through the forest. The dagger warmed itself against his chest, and underneath liberty pounded, hidden close. A lustful, panting dialogue raced down the pages like a rivulet of snakes, and one felt it had been decided from eternity. Even to those caresses which writhed about the lover's body, as though wishing to keep him there, to dissuade him from it; they sketched abominably the frame of that other body it was necessary to destroy. Nothing had been forgotten: alibis, unforeseen hazards, possible mistakes. From this hour on, each instant had its use minutely assigned. The cold-blooded, twice-gone-over re-examination of the details was barely broken off so that a hand could caress a cheek. It was beginning to get dark.

Not looking at one another now, rigidly fixed upon the task which awaited them, they separated at the cabin door. She was to follow the trail that led north. On the path leading in the opposite direction, he turned for a moment to watch her running, her hair loosened and flying. He ran in turn, crouching among the trees and hedges until, in the yellowish fog of dusk, he could distinguish the avenue of trees which led up to the house. The dogs were not supposed to bark, they did not bark. The estate manager would not be there at this hour, and he was not there. He went up the three porch steps and entered. The woman's words reached him over the thudding of blood in his ears: first a blue chamber, then a hall, then a carpeted stairway. At the top, two doors. No one in the first room, no one in the second. The door of the salon, and then, the knife in hand, the light from the great windows, the high back of an armchair covered in green velvet, the head of the man in the chair reading a novel.

JERZY KOSINSKI (1933–)
WAS BORN IN POLAND.
HE NOW LIVES IN THE
UNITED STATES AND IS
BEST KNOWN FOR HIS
NOVEL *BEING THERE*.
HE SPEAKS FIVE
LANGUAGES, AND HIS
STYLE IS OFTEN STARK
AND BRUTAL IN ITS
DESCRIPTION OF
HUMAN BEHAVIOUR.
KOSINSKI IS ALSO A
WRITER OF LYRICAL
AND COMIC FICTION,
BUT HIS NOVELS, SUCH
AS *THE PAINTED BIRD*,
OFTEN DEAL WITH THE
CRUELTIES OF WAR AND
DEVASTATION.

STEPS
(excerpt)

Jerzy Kosinski

There were several of us, all archeological assistants, working on one of the islands with a professor who for years had been excavating remnants of an ancient civilization that had flourished fifteen centuries before our era.

It was an advanced civilization, the professor claimed, but at some point a massive catastrophe had wiped it out. He had challenged the prevailing theory that a disastrous earthquake, followed by a tidal wave, had struck the island. We were collecting fragments of pottery, sifting through ashes for the remains of artifacts, and unearthing building materials, all of which the professor catalogued as evidence to support his as yet unpublished work.

After a month I decided to leave the excavations and visit a neighboring island. In my haste to catch the ferry I left without my paycheck, but I obtained the promise that it would be forwarded on the next mail skiff. I could live for one day on the money I had with me.

After arriving I spent the entire day sightseeing. The island was dominated by a dormant volcano, its broad slopes covered with porous lava rock, weathered to form a poor but arable soil.

I walked down to the harbor; an hour before sunset, when the air was cooling, the fishing boats put out for the night. I watched them slide over the calm, almost waveless water until their long, low forms vanished from sight. The islands suddenly lost the light reflected from their rocky spines and grew stark and black. And then, as though drawn silently beneath the surface, they disappeared one by one.

On the morning of the second day I went down to the quay to meet the mail skiff. To my consternation my paycheck had not arrived. I stood on the dock, wondering how I was going to live and whether I would even be able to leave the island. A few fishermen sat by their nets, watching me; they sensed that something was wrong. Three of them approached and spoke to me. Not understanding, I replied in the two languages I knew: their faces became sullen and hostile, and they abruptly turned away. That evening I took my sleeping bag down to the beach and slept on the sand.

In the morning I spent the last of my money on a cup of coffee. After strolling up the winding streets behind the port, I walked through the scrubby fields to the nearest village. The villagers sat in the shade, covertly watching me. Hungry and thirsty, I returned to the beach again, walking beneath a blazing sun. I had nothing to barter for food or money: no watch, no fountain pen, no cuff links, no camera, no wallet. At noon, when the sun stood high and the villagers sheltered in their cottages, I went to the police station. I found the island's solitary policeman dozing by the telephone. I woke him, but he seemed reluctant to understand even my simplest gesture. I pointed to his phone, pulling out my empty pockets; I made signs and drew pictures, even miming thirst and hunger. All this had no effect: the policeman showed neither interest nor understanding, and the phone remained locked. It was the only one on the island; the guidebook I had read had even bothered to note the fact.

In the afternoon I strolled around the village, smiling at the inhabitants, hoping to be offered a drink or to be invited to a meal. No one returned my greeting; the villagers turned away and the storekeepers simply ignored me. The church was on the largest island of the group and I had no means of getting there to ask for food and shelter. I returned to the beach as if expecting help to rise up from the sea. I was famished and exhausted. The sun had brought on a pounding headache, I felt waves of vertigo. Unexpectedly I caught the sound of people talking in an alien language. Turning, I saw two women sitting close to the water. Folds of gray, heavily veined fat hung from their thighs and upper arms; their full, pendulous breasts were squashed in outsize brassieres.

They sunbathed sprawling on their beach towels surrounded by picnic equipment: food baskets, thermos flasks, parasols, and nets full of fruit. A pile of books, heaped up alongside, conspicuously displayed library numbers. They were evidently tourists staying with a local family. I approached them slowly but directly, anxious not to alarm them. They stopped talking, and I greeted them smilingly, using my languages in turn. They replied in another one. We had no common language, but I was very conscious of the proximity of food. I sat down beside them as though I had understood I had been invited. When they began to eat I eyed the food; they either did not notice this or ignored my intense stare. After a few minutes the woman I judged to be the older offered me an apple. I ate it slowly, trying to conceal my hunger and hoping for something more solid. They watched me intently.

It was hot on the beach and I dozed off. But I woke when the two women pulled themselves to their feet, their shoulders and back red from the sun. Rivulets of perspiration streaked the sand that clung to their flabby thighs, the fat slid over their hips as they braced themselves to stoop and collect their belongings. I helped them. With flirtatious nods they set off along the inner rim of the beach; I followed.

We reached the house they occupied. On entering I was hit by another wave of vertigo; I stumbled on a step and collapsed. Laughing and chattering, the women undressed me and maneuvered me onto a large, low bed. Still dazed, I pointed to my stomach. There was no delay: they rushed to bring me meat, fruit, and milk. Before I could finish the meal, they had drawn the curtains and torn off their bathing suits. Naked, they fell upon me. I was buried beneath their heavy bellies and broad backs; my arms were pinioned; my body was manipulated squeezed, pressed, and thumped.

I was at the dock at dawn. The mail skiff came in, but there was neither a check nor a letter for me. I stood there watching the boat recede into the hot sun that dissolved the morning mist, revealing one by one the distant islands.

SHORT SHORT MANUAL

◆

CREATIVE EXERCISES

1. **ASSUME YOU DIED TODAY.** Write your own obituary in the style of Richard Brautigan's "The World War I Los Angeles Airplane."

2. **FIND A PARTNER IN YOUR CLASS.** Read "The Upturned Face" as if the dead man were your partner. Write about your feelings. Would you react in the same way that the soldier did?

3. **CHOOSE ONE OF THE STORIES IN THE BOOK.** Assume that it does not end where it now ends, because part of the author's original manuscript was lost. You are required to write a sequel, a last line, a last paragraph, or a completely new section. How do you think the story should end? Try this same idea with the beginning of a story: what happened before the story began?

4. **READ ONLY THE BEGINNING AND ENDING OF ONE OF THE STORIES.** Then write the middle yourself.

5. **TAKE A SCENE OR SECTION FROM ONE OF THE STORIES AND TURN IT INTO A** dramatic dialogue between the characters.

6. **READ L. P. HARTLEY'S "A HIGH DIVE."** Assume that you are an employer who must hire a new worker. Write a character profile and a letter of recommendation (or refusal) on the high diver based on what the story tells you about his character.

7. **"SAYING GOOD-BYE TO TOM"** is told from several points of view. Read "The Fourth Alarm" and re-tell the story from the wife's point of view. Try this with another story of your own choosing.

8. **READ DORIS LESSING'S "A ROOM."** Write something in the same manner about your own room.

9. **READ "KEEPING FIT," "MARY," AND "THE MAN WHO LOVED FLOWERS"** and write a letter to the central character telling what you think about him or her. Write a letter to the author of any story and tell him or her what you think of his or her story.

10. **AS A PARENT, WHAT WOULD YOU SAY TO THE BOY IN "CHARLES"?**

11. **"THIS STORY HAD ONE FOOT IN THE GRAVE AND THE OTHER ON A BANANA PEEL.** It should have died with the runner." This was one student's response to Matt Cohen's "Keeping Fit." Why do you think the student felt that way? How do you feel about the story?

12. **SELECT AND READ A BOOK REVIEW FROM A MAGAZINE OR NEWSPAPER.** Note some of the techniques the reviewer uses. Read one of the stories as if it had just been published, and write a newspaper review on its content, style, and relevance.

13. **READ ANY ONE OF THE FOLLOWING:** "Pierrette's Bumps," "When Greek Meets Greek," "Mary," "The Kissing Man," or "The Prodigal Parent." Take the lead character in the story and write a comparison with a person you know who is similar to that character.

14. **SELECT ANY CHARACTER FROM ONE OF THE STORIES.** In the voice of that character, write five successive diary entries that correspond to the time during which the story takes place.

15. **HOW MANY OF THESE STORIES DO YOU THINK COULD BE MADE INTO A** successful movie or TV series? Explain your reasons and write a script outline describing the major scenes. Cast the roles, with either well-known performers or your classmates.

SUGGESTIONS FOR STUDY

The following exercises ask you to read a group of stories and compare their use of theme, characterization, and narrative devices.

THEME

1. **LOOK AT ALL THE STORIES IN EACH OF THE FIVE SECTIONS OF THE BOOK AND** compare their central themes. Each section is arranged according to one unifying idea; try to determine specifically how each author explores the unifying idea.

2. **THE FOLLOWING STORIES ALL DEAL,** in one way or another, with love: "The Kissing Man," "The Man Who Loved Flowers," "Bridal Suite," "The Prodigal Parent," and "Whole." Compare and contrast how the authors deal with love.

3. **HOW DOES EACH AUTHOR TREAT THE THEME OF COMING OF AGE IN THE** following stories: "Pierrette's Bumps," "Up in Michigan," and "The Turtle"?

4. **IN WHAT WAYS ARE THE FOLLOWING STORIES HUMOROUS:** "The Parrot," "When Greek Meets Greek," "The Elephant," and "Bug-Getter"?

CHARACTERIZATION

1. **IN WHAT DIFFERENT WAYS ARE THE MAIN CHARACTERS IN THE FOLLOWING** stories isolated from society: "Billy the Kid," "A Room," "Mary," "Pierrette's Bumps," "Charles," and "The Fourth Alarm"?

2. **HOW ARE THE LEAD CHARACTERS IN THE FOLLOWING STORIES AT ODDS WITH THE** people they live and work with: "My Life with R. H. Macy," "A High Dive," "The Fourth Alarm," "Steps," and "The Kissing Man"?

3. **TRY TO PINPOINT THE MAJOR MOTIVATIONS OF EACH OF THE CENTRAL** characters in these stories: "A High Dive," "Up in Michigan," "The World War I Los Angeles Airplane," and "Heil!"?

4. **IN WHAT SPECIFIC WAYS DO THE MINOR CHARACTERS IN THE FOLLOWING STORIES** affect the actions and feelings of the major characters: "The Fourth Alarm," "6550," "The Prodigal Parent," "The Use of Force," and "1912: The Bridge Beginning"?

NARRATIVE DEVICES

*Dialogue, point of view, structure, and openings and closings are
narrative devices. Examine the use of each device in the stories listed
after each one.*

1. **DIALOGUE:** "When Greek Meets Greek," "Bridal Suite," "Saying Good-bye to Tom,"
"The Prodigal Parent," and "Pierrette's Bumps."

2. **POINT OF VIEW:** "Keeping Fit," "6550," "A Room," "Mary," "Snow," and "The World
War I Los Angeles Airplane."

3. **STRUCTURE:** "Mary," "1912: The Bridge Beginning," "Mariana," "Continuity of Parks,"
"The Gunfighter," and "Saying Good-bye to Tom."

4. **OPENINGS AND CLOSINGS:** "The Man Who Loved Flowers," "Saying Good-bye to Tom,"
"The Blue Bouquet," "Bug-Getter," and "Heil!"

RAYMOND CARVER IS
THE AUTHOR OF TWO
COLLECTIONS OF
SHORT STORIES, "WILL
YOU PLEASE BE QUIET,
PLEASE?" AND THE
FORTHCOMING "WHAT
WE TALK ABOUT WHEN
WE TALK ABOUT LOVE."
HE IS A PROFESSOR OF
ENGLISH IN THE
WRITING PROGRAM OF
SYRACUSE UNIVERSITY.

A STORYTELLER'S SHOPTALK

Raymond Carver

When I was 27, back in 1966, I found I was having trouble concentrating my attention on long narrative fiction. For a time I experienced difficulty in trying to read it as well as in attempting to write it. My attention span had gone out on me; I no longer had the patience to try to write novels. It's an involved story, too tedious to talk about here. But I know it has much to do now with why I write poems and short stories. Get in, get out. Don't linger. Go on. It could be that I lost any great ambitions at about the same time, in my late 20's. If I did, I think it was good it happened. Ambition and a little luck are good things for a writer to have going for him. Too much ambition and bad luck, or no luck at all, can be killing. There has to be talent.

Some writers have a bunch of talent; I don't know any writers who are without it. But a unique and exact way of looking at things, and finding the right context for expressing that way of looking, that's something else. "The World According to Garp" is of course the marvelous world according to John Irving. There is another world according to Flannery O'Connor, and others according to William Faulkner and Ernest Hemingway. There are worlds according to Cheever, Updike, Singer, Stanley Elkin, Ann Beattie, Cynthia Ozick, Donald Barthelme, Mary Robison, William Kittredge, Barry Hannah. Every great or even every very good writer makes the world over according to his own specifications.

It's akin to style, what I'm talking about, but it isn't style alone. It is the writer's particular and unmistakable signature on everything he writes. It is his world and no other. This is one of the things that distinguishes one writer from another. Not talent. There's plenty of that around. But a writer who has some special way of looking at things and who gives artistic expression to that way of looking: that writer may be around for a time.

Isak Dinesen said that she wrote a little every day, without hope and without despair. Someday I'll put that on a three-by-five card and tape it to the wall beside my desk. I have some three-by-five cards on the wall now. "Fundamental accuracy of statement is the ONE sole morality of writing." Ezra Pound. It is not everything by ANY means, but if a writer has "fundamental accuracy of statement" going for him, he's at least on the right track.

I have a three-by-five up there with this fragment of a sentence from a story by Chekhov: "...and suddenly everything became clear to him." I find these words filled with wonder and possibility. I love their simple clarity, and the hint of revelation that is implied. There is a bit of mystery, too. What has been unclear before? Why is it just now becoming clear? What's happened? Most of all —what now? There are consequences as a result of such sudden awakenings. I feel a sharp sense of relief—and anticipation.

I overheard the writer Geoffrey Wolff say "No cheap tricks" to a group of writing students. That should go on a three-by-five card. I'd amend it a little to "No tricks." Period. I hate tricks. At the first sign of a trick or a gimmick in a piece of fiction, a cheap trick or even an elaborate trick, I tend to look for cover. Tricks are ultimately boring, and I get bored easily, which may go along with my not having much of an attention span. But extremely clever chi-chi writing, or just plain tomfoolery writing, puts me to sleep. Writers don't need tricks or gimmicks or even necessarily need to be the smartest fellows on the block. At the risk of appearing foolish, a writer sometimes needs to be able to just stand and gape at this or that thing—a sunset or an old shoe—in absolute and simple amazement.

Some months ago, in this Book Review, John Barth said that 10 years ago most of the students in his fiction writing seminar were interested in "formal innovation," and this no longer seems to be the case. He's a little worried that writers are going to start writing mom and pop novels in the 1980's. He worries that experimentation may be on the way out, along with liberalism. I get a little nervous if I find myself within earshot of somber discussion about "formal innovation" in fiction writing. Too often "experimentation" is a license to be careless, silly or imitative in the writing. Even worse, a license to try to brutalize or alienate the reader. Too often such writing gives us no news of the world, or else describes a desert landscape and that's all—a few dunes and lizards here and there, but no people; a place uninhabited by anything recognizably human, a place of interest only to a few scientific specialists.

It should be noted that real experiment in fiction is original, hard-earned and cause for rejoicing. But someone else's way of looking at things—Barthelme's, for instance—should not be chased after by other writers. It won't work. There is only one Barthelme, and for another writer to try to appropriate Barthelme's peculiar sensibility or *mise en scène* under the rubric of innovation is for that writer to mess around with chaos and disaster and, worse, self-deception. The real experimenters have to Make It New, as Pound urged, and in the process have to find things out for themselves. But if writers haven't taken leave of their senses, they also want to stay in touch with us, they want to carry news from their world to ours.

It's possible, in a poem or a short story, to write about commonplace things and objects using commonplace but precise language, and to endow those things —a chair, a window curtain, a fork, a stone, a woman's earrings—with immense, even startling power. It is possible to write a line of seemingly innocuous dialogue and have it send a chill along the reader's spine—the source of artistic delight, as Nabokov would have it. That's the kind of writing that most interests me. I hate sloppy or haphazard writing whether it flies under the banner of experimentation or else is just clumsily rendered realism. In Isaac Babel's wonderful short story, "Guy de Maupassant," the narrator has this to say about the writing of fiction: "No iron can pierce the heart with such force as a period put just at the right place." This too ought to go on a three-by-five.

Evan Connell said once that he knew he was finished with a short story when he found himself going through it and taking out commas and then going through the story again and putting commas back in the same places. I like that way of working on something. I respect that kind of care for what is being done. That's all we have, finally, the words, and they had better be the right ones, with the punctuation in the right places so that they can best say what they are meant to say. If the words are heavy with the writer's own unbridled emotions, or if they are imprecise and inaccurate for some other reason—if the words are in any way blurred—the reader's eyes will slide right over them and nothing will be achieved. The reader's own artistic sense will simply not be engaged. Henry James called this sort of hapless writing "weak specification."

I have friends who've told me they had to hurry a book because they needed the money, their editor or their wife was leaning on them or leaving them—something, some apology for the writing not being very good. "It would have been better if I'd taken the time." I was dumbfounded when I heard a novelist friend say this. I still am, if I think about it, which I don't. It's none of my business. But if the writing can't be made as good as it is within us to make it, then why do it? In the end it's all we have, the only thing we can take into the grave. I wanted to say to my friend, for heaven's sake go do something else. There have to be easier and maybe more honest ways to try and earn a living. Or else just do it to the best of your abilities, your talents, and then don't justify or make excuses. Don't complain, don't explain.

In an essay called, simply enough, "Writing Short Stories," Flannery O'Connor talks about writing as an act of discovery. O'Connor says she most often did not know where she was going when she sat down to work on a short story. She says she doubts that many writers know where they are going when they begin something. She uses "Good Country People" as an example of how she put together a short story whose ending she could not even guess at until she was nearly there:

"When I started writing that story, I didn't know there was going to be a Ph.D. with a wooden leg in it. I merely found myself one morning writing a description of two women I knew something about, and before I realized it, I had equipped one of them with a daughter with a wooden leg. I brought in the Bible salesman, but I had no idea what I was going to do with him. I didn't know he was going to steal that wooden leg until ten or twelve lines before he did it, but when I found out that this was what was going to happen, I realized it was inevitable."

When I read this some years ago it came as a shock that she, or anyone for that matter, wrote stories in this fashion. I thought this was my uncomfortable secret, and I was just a little uneasy with it. For sure I thought this way of working on a short story somehow revealed my own shortcomings. I remember being tremendously heartened by reading what she had to say on the subject.

I once sat down to write what turned out to be a pretty good story, though only the first sentence of the story had offered itself to me when I began it. For several days I'd been going around with this sentence in my head: "He was running the vacuum cleaner when the telephone rang." I knew a story was there and that it wanted telling. I felt it in my bones, that a story belonged with that beginning, if I could just have the time to write it. I found the time, an entire day —twelve, fifteen hours even—if I wanted to make use of it. I did, and I sat down in the morning and wrote the first sentence, and other sentences promptly began to attach themselves. I made the story just as I'd make a poem; one line and then the next, and the next. Pretty soon I could see a story, and I knew it was my story, the one I'd been wanting to write.

I like it when there is some feeling of threat or sense of menace in short stories. I think a little menace is fine to have in a story. For one thing, it's good for the circulation. There has to be tension, a sense that something is imminent, that certain things are in relentless motion, or else, most often, there simply won't be a story. What creates tension in a piece of fiction is partly the way the concrete words are linked together to make up the visible action of the story. But it's also the things that are left out, that are implied, the landscape just under the smooth (but sometimes broken and unsettled) surface of things.

V. S. Pritchett's definition of a short story is "something glimpsed from the corner of the eye, in passing." Notice the "glimpse" part of this. First the glimpse. Then the glimpse given life, turned into something that illuminates the moment and may, if we're lucky—that word again—have even further-ranging consequences and meaning. The short story writer's task is to invest the glimpse with all that is in his power. He'll bring his intelligence and literary skill to bear (his talent), his sense of proportion and sense of the fitness of things; of how things out there really are and how he sees those things—like no one else sees them. And this is done through the use of clear and specific language, language used so as to bring to life the details that will light up the story for the reader. For the details to be concrete and convey meaning, the language must be accurate and precisely given. The words can be so precise they may even sound flat, but they can still carry; if used right, they can hit all the notes.
